W. R. Neale

Time the Avenger

and other poems

W. R. Neale

Time the Avenger
and other poems

ISBN/EAN: 9783337406509

Printed in Europe, USA, Canada, Australia, Japan

Cover: Foto ©Andreas Hilbeck / pixelio.de

More available books at **www.hansebooks.com**

TIME THE AVENGER,

AND

Other Poems.

BY

W. R. NEALE.

LONDON:
W. KENT & CO., PATERNOSTER ROW.
BARNSTAPLE: CORNISH.
1860.

TO

THE RIGHT HONOURABLE

THE EARL FORTESCUE, K.G., ETC., ETC.,

THIS SMALL

VOLUME OF POEMS

IS BY PERMISSION

RESPECTFULLY INSCRIBED

BY HIS LORDSHIP'S MOST OBEDIENT SERVANT,

THE AUTHOR.

Instow, North Devon,
July, 1860.

DEDICATION.

———◆———

CHIEF of a race! whose sires bequeathed to thee
A heritage of true patrician worth,
Greater than all the titles which had birth
When the first Norman conqueror crossed the sea;
Who stood, when freedom's friends were factious called,
Foremost amidst the bold undaunted few,
Until the state from rank corruption grew
Pure, and from grievous errors disenthralled;
To thee, with years and ripe experience crowned,
Giving wise counsel in the hour of need,
And ever, with prompt aid and noble deed,
In the vanguard at duty's summons found,
I dedicate these lays, whose homely sound,
Lacking the point and polish of the schools,
May jar on ears attuned by learning's rules,
And in the critic's mystic art profound:
Yet know I, should this rude uncultured song
Call forth one honest tear for mortal woe,
Or bid the listener's breast indignant glow
With generous sympathy for human wrong,
That, though the theme might claim an abler tongue
Than his, who these unskilful notes hath sung,
The bard, who now awakes this feeble strain,
Has touched his lyre not lightly nor in vain.

CONTENTS.

TIME THE AVENGER.

TIME THE AVENGER.

The ages gather and the world grows grey,
And seasons come and go; night follows day,
And day receding night; the moments speed,
Ever upon the wing, and take no heed,
How, in the course of swift departing years,
Man reaps his heritage of toil and tears;
Pursues on glory's track the distant prize,
Whose fleeting image mocks him as it flies,
Or climbs the perilous steep that leads to fame,
To build beyond oblivion's reach a name;
Or flushed with hope, or pallid with despair,
Drinks the alternate cup of joy and care,
Blown by the winds, the sport of every wave,
His only resting place on earth—the grave.
And nations, empires, kingdoms, pass away,
Art's loftiest triumphs reared by hands of clay,

The marble palace and the solemn fane,
The hundred-gated city of the plain,
The schools where listening youth enraptured hung,
On words of eloquence from wisdom's tongue,
The busy mart, the forum with its throng,
Arch, column, circus, temple—all, save song,
Which lives unfading, changeless, and sublime,
Yield to thy ruthless hand, avenging Time!

In vain laborious science would explore,
The fossil prints of races now no more,
The crumbling skeletons of things that were
The monster denizens of sea and air,
Before the mountains rose from out the flood,
Or earth adorned with blossom and with bud,
First greeted him, the ruler of the rest,
Creation's noblest work, her last and best.
The sage still trims and wastes his midnight oil,
In deep research and unavailing toil,
Fain would he learn when first from chaos came,
Out of the shapeless mass, this wondrous frame,
Stars, suns, and systems, that revolving glow,
Filling all space—around, above, below;

Would ask, if in these orbs, whose course we trace,
Some higher type of being finds a place,
Breathing, more blest than we, a purer air,
In fields more fragrant and in climes more fair,
A glorious destiny, all light within,
Untouched by error and unstained by sin ;
Or if in barren grandeur, stretched immense,
Mere matter spread above the grasp of sense,
These planets, fashioned by a hand divine,
Roll on uncultured and unpeopled shine :
But not to finite reason can be known,
What forms exist in spheres beyond our own,
The weak attempt that would the mystery scan,
In mere conjecture, ends where it began ;
Then, less presumptuous grown, and taught to see,
The baffled flight of man's philosophy,
To earth returning, still he seeks to trace,
Some vestige of the story of his race ;
Would pierce the mist of vanished centuries,
Which veil the shadowy past from mortal eyes,
And learn in what primeval hour went forth,
The first frail bark that reached the frozen north,
To plant the dwarfed, degenerate Esquimaux,
In that wild region of untrodden snow;

Would ask what power unseen, what unknown hand,
Could tempt his steps to that inclement strand,
In dreary solitudes, with tempests rife,
To battle with the elements for life,
Where barren rocks beneath a polar sky,
And withered wastes his nurture scarce supply,
Yet in the shelter of his seal-skin tent,
Deeming his lot luxurious, is content,
And thinks, in that inhospitable zone,
No other land so lovely as his own.
Again, inquiring reason would be told,
What spirit led the mariner of old,
What syren lured with her enchanting strain,
His slim canoe across the Indian main,
What instinct could that ancient wanderer guide,
A thousand leagues athwart the pathless tide,
To find, upon those fair and fabled isles,
A home, where gorgeous summer ceaseless smiles,
Where lavish nature, from her coral caves,
A second Eden forms amidst the waves,
Where grow spontaneous from the teeming soil,
Fruits that tax not the weary hand of toil,
And all the flowers successive seasons bring,
Bloom with the verdure of perpetual spring.

Is there no star whose gleam our course can light,
Back through the past's impenetrable night,
To learn whence spread o'er realms and regions vast,
The varied types of colour, creed, and caste?
The roving son of Araby the blest,
The savage in his prairie of the West,
The Nubian, darkened by the tropic's glow,
The Arctic hunter in his hut of snow,
Tribe, sect, and nation, family, and clan,
To fill their place in the appointed plan?
Idly we ask, on Lethe's wreck-strewn shore,
Tradition's feeble torch reveals no more,
Than ruins, cankered by Oblivion's rust,
Time's mouldering records chronicled in dust!
And so, when genius hails the distant height,
The far horizon of his bounded sight,
And thinks, the towering summit once attained,
All knowledge mastered, and all wisdom gained;
Yet, through a life-long scorn of sloth and sleep,
Standing triumphant on the mist-clad steep,
Behold! what prospects fill his wondering eyes,
New plains extend, and other mountains rise,
And far beyond, magnificently lone,
The wide, wide sea, unfathomed and unknown!

And such the mere epitome, the span,
And fragment of existence given to man ;
Enough, a little of the past to see,
Some glimpses of a future destiny,
The present evil intermixed with good,
The lot unequal, weakly understood,
To search for truth, and only reach the shore
Of that vast ocean, rolling evermore,
Beneath the billows of whose sleepless breast,
Caverned in depths profound, her hidden treasures rest.

And wheresoe'er our wandering footsteps tread,
Amidst the silent cities of the dead,
There, brooding o'er corruption and decay,
Sits desolation as a bird of prey,
Beneath whose glance, blent in a common doom,
The prostrate pillar and the shattered tomb,
Are mingled with the wrecks of former things,
The shrines of priests, and palaces of kings.
Then marvel we upon the marge of Nile,
What Titan hand upraised the ponderous pile,
Or poised the massive obelisk, which still
Mocks at the modern's imitative skill ;

What hand forgotten, and what art unknown,

Carved the huge sphinx from out the shapeless stone,

When infant science in a darkened age,

First claimed the culture of the Memphian sage,

To light progressive nations yet to come,

When Ethiopia's voices should be dumb,

And nought, of all the Pharaohs and their thrones,

Stand, save the sepulchres that shroud their bones.

And she, the elder born, but not the less

Renowned, chief city of the wilderness,

Chaldea's glory, pride of all the earth,

Loud was her heathen song of midnight mirth ;

The jewelled wine-cup sparkled in her halls,

A thousand lamps shone on her sculptured walls,

Yet, in the midst of that voluptuous strain,

For her the watchman wakened but in vain ;

Mysterious fingers trace her coming fate,

The fiery Persian thunders at her gate,

To-day victorious, but in turn to yield

To him who bore the Macedonian shield,

Until a greater conqueror than he,

Ruler of all that hath been, and shall be,

Should give to devastation's ruthless sway,
The golden idol with its feet of clay.
And thou! whose commerce filled the peopled streets,
Whose merchants were thy princes, and whose fleets,
Impelled by conquest, or allured by gain,
Rich freighted filled the unfrequented main;
Daughter of Sidon! in thine hour of joy,
Rare were thy gifts and many, thou didst cloy
Thy marts with all the treasures earth could yield,
Adventurous won from forest, mine, and field,
And royally in thy Tyrian robe arrayed,
The gladdened isles beheld thee and obeyed;
All nations at thy footstool tribute gave,
For thou wert throned the mistress of the wave!
Then came thy tribulation and thy shame,
Nothing of thee remaineth but thy name,
We ask thy place in vain,——thou art no more,
The sea thou ruledst answereth evermore,
And in the hollow sounding of the surge,
We hear at once thy record and thy dirge!

Know ye a clime, immortal in her age,
Where rose the bard, the hero, and the sage,

Where every plain recalls a battle won,

And every shore some proud achievement done ;

Whence sprung, divinest power to mortals taught,

The arts that give eternity to thought,

And beauteous shapes and noble deeds prolong,

In matchless sculpture and unrivalled song ?

There,—though the Delphian oracle be mute,

And still the breathings of the Doric flute,

Though fled the forms that filled the poet's dreams,

From thyme-clad mountains and Arcadian streams ;

Though shaft and urn by war and tempest reft,

Are all decay's effacing touch hath left,

Where still in solitary grandeur stands,

Some fane dismantled by barbarian hands ;

Yet, changeless, on the listener's ravished ear,

Falls the old strain, impassioned, full, and clear,

Which Scio's sightless bard enraptured sung

To Greece, when time and all the world were young :

And from these ashes gleams a living fire,

To warm the breast of him who would aspire,

A voice which bids the soul that dare be free,

Tread thy wild pass, renowned Thermopylæ !

And standing fearless on the Spartan's grave,

Unsheath the sword and be no more a slave !

And even thus, from this unequalled shore,
Famous in arms and rife with ancient lore,
Where Plato's spirit lingers as the light,
Which dwells at sunset on Colonna's height;
The unrelenting tide has swept at last,
All but the mighty shadows of the past,
Gigantic phantoms rising from the gloom,
Wan spectres of her greatness and her doom.

And thou! whose power a prostrate world subdued,
Before whose feet the vanquished nations sued,
Imperial Rome! loud was thy people's cry,
As marched the toil-worn legions stately by,
When they, exulting from the crimson track
Of conquest, bore thine eagle standards back,
Crowned with the honours of successful war,
The laurel wreath, the proud triumphal car,
While captive monarchs filled that pageant high,
Yoked to the chariot wheels of victory!
Yet thine were triumphs greater than the sway
Of empires won in battle's fierce array,
When lured to death by what the world calls fame,
Ambition's madmen play their reckless game,

And men by millions perish in their gore,
To make some despot's state one realm the more!
To thee and to thy gifted sons belong,
Arts, commerce, language, liberty, and song!
The sculptor's skill beneath whose chisel grew,
Those shapes to nature so divinely true,
They seem to ask one spark from heaven alone,
To quicken into life the breathless stone,
And with the true Promethean fire supply,
Speech to the lips and lightning to the eye!
Thine argosies by every breeze were fanned,
Laden with spoils from many a subject land,
And thine the fervent tongue which did inspire,
Impetuous thoughts writ with a pen of fire,
And strains which through remotest years unfold,
Texts for the young and watchwords for the old!
And they survive the Coliseum's fall,
Arch, circus, aqueduct, and shattered wall,
Where idly grows the rank luxuriant weed,
O'er the fallen altars of a vanished creed,
Upon whose wrecks a newer faith appeared,
By priests perverted and their dupes revered;
Whose power, upheld in blood, and grief, and tears,
And homage wrung from superstition's fears,

In outworn impotence would yet essay,
To quench the dawning of that perfect day,
When Truth indignant rends the bonds in twain,
Which still this darkened universe enchain,
Thick mists which o'er the bigot's pathway roll,
To blind the reason and enslave the soul.
Lo! standing radiant on yon Alpine height,
The white-robed herald of approaching light,
Invokes the spirit of the olden days,
That filled anew the Tuscan poet's lays,
And roused the artist, sculptor, engineer,
When Florence trembled at the foeman's spear,
To wield with equal force the sword or pen,
And teach, inspire, and lead his fellow men :
Which yet, in minds predestined to be free,
From Tiber to the Adriatic sea,
Finds utterance, treading down as idle things,
The creeds of monks and policies of kings,
And bids a breathless world expectant wait,
The climax of their country's coming fate,
When the long-gathered thunder-cloud shall break,
And earth's dominions to their centre shake ;
When Time in retribution's hour shall close,
The weary story of her wrongs and woes,

Bidding ennobled manhood walk secure,
In noontide gleam of laws made just and pure,
And Freedom, as eternal as the fame,
That gilds the records of her ancient name.

Thus glides the ceaseless current silently,
On which the world's great drama passes by,
Drawn by the force of Fate's resistless laws,
The constant sequence of effect and cause ;
States rise and fall, the strongest rules the rest,
By turns oppressing, and in turn opprest ;
Jew, Christian, Moslem, hold alternate sway,
Act out their destined part, and pass away ;
Earth's dynasties presumptuous reach the sky,
Grow great, luxurious, ripen, fade, and die ;
The statesman plies his craft while justice sleeps,
Zeal apes devotion, and religion weeps ;
Mock patriots clam'rous for mankind's applause,
Wax feebly fervent in their country's cause,
And take, reluctant—could we trust the face—
The pay that constitutes the charm of place ;
Indignant merit, virtuously poor,
Eyes the vain crowd that throng at Dives' door,

Who, deaf to sorrow's supplicating groan,
Recks of no mortal suffering save his own ;
And to the stern primeval mandate true,
Which makes the many vassals for the few,
With hand unsparing, and with breast grown cold,
Buys, sells, and barters, pauper blood for gold :
And genius, lacking wealth and worldly store,
Full of rich attributes, yet ever poor,
Thin-robed and thorn-crowned in the great highways,
Unapprehended by the vulgar gaze,
Fulfils his mission, finds an early grave,
And then, too late to succour or to save,
Men heap elaborate honours o'er the head
Of him, who living, asked in vain for bread !

Ye gilded moths who flutter in the ray
Of fashion's summer, indolently gay,
Who heed not in your painted plumage drest,
The weary fingers and the broken rest
Of her, who plies the needle o'er and o'er,
To give embroidered pride one grace the more ;
Who midst the round of pleasure callous grown,
Think not of those whose pillow is the stone,

Who, foodless and forsaken, watch and weep,
While you on silken cushions tranquil sleep :
Say! why has Fortune's partial hand allowed
To you the sunshine and to them the cloud?
To you full meed of corn and wine and oil,
To them the thorn, the thistle, and the toil?
The daily cares that on misfortune wait,
The apprehension of to-morrow's fate,
And dread of poverty's unnumbered woes,
Whose shadows deepen at the journey's close?
Wherefore! are ye more just, or wise, or pure,
That they alone should suffer and endure?
And dare ye answer—that the griefs they bear,
Which plough deep furrows in the brow of care,
Which drive the bloom from youthful cheeks too soon,
And quench the fire of manhood ere his noon,
Are self-sought evils born of want and sin,
The natural fruit of hearts corrupt within?
Or will ye reconcile conflicting rules,
Taught by the purblind masters of the schools,
That man can combat of his own free will,
The torrent of predestinated ill?
Or, leaning helpless on a broken reed,
Wrecked upon Calvin's cold unchristian creed,

Shall he surrender faith's delusive trust,

And cry—I yield to fate; what must be, *must ?*

Which of the twain can heal the broken heart,

Nerve the weak arm and newer zeal impart ?

Can either check the unavailing sigh,

Fresh strength bestow and teach us how to die?

Behold the labourer's doom !   From day to day,

He slaves while Mammon doles the scanty pay,

He gives his youth's best days, his manhood's strength,

Till age o'ertakes the worn-out frame at length ;

Then, when you 've done with him, his spade and flail,

There frowns the workhouse, or there yawns the jail,

Or darker lot, in climes beyond the wave,

A felon's exile and a convict's grave.

Now while the rude wind shakes yon broken pane,

Through which thick beats the chill December rain,

The man of sorrows on his meagre bed,

In mortal anguish rests the languid head ;

No gentle hand, no kindly voice is there,

In that dark home of famine and despair ;

Yet marvel not,——he lays without a frown,

The weary burden of existence down,

And calmly reading, with unquailing look,

The last sad page of life's eventful book,

Hails the behest that sets his spirit free,
As hope's first gleam of immortality;
Then, vainly seek the powers of death and hell,
The ransomed soul's omnipotence to quell;
Thus, through the terrors of the shadowy vale,
While demon shapes her onward course assail,
Rings midst the gloom her proud triumphant cry,
Where is thy sting? grave! where thy victory?

I stood within the modern Babylon,
In the wan beam of drear November's sun;
That city huge, whose traffic chokes the street,
Mart of the world, where many nations meet,
Where pours from morn till eve the eager throng,
And ceaseless stream of human life along:
A voiceless, breathless multitude were there,
And ever and anon the misty air
Grew heavy with the deep-toned frequent bell,
Tolling a mighty warrior's funeral knell:
Then came a vast procession, and the beat
Of muffled drums, and measured tramp of feet,
And bearded veterans passed in many a band,
Princes and chiefs and rulers of the land;

For he they bore upon his lofty bier,
In bannered pomp with helm and plume and spear,
Was England's greatest soldier in his day,
In peril's hour her safeguard and her stay ;
A man of high resolve and iron will,
Armed ever ready at approaching ill,
In court or camp to follow or to lead,
Where duty prompted at his country's need ;
And full of wealth, renown, and length of days,
By all men known with reverent love and praise,
They laid him in the grandeur and the gloom,
Of that great temple rich with many a tomb,
Round which is heard the busy city's roar,
As seas that sound upon our island shore ;
With all his worldly honours,—dust to dust,
To wait the resurrection of the just :
And then that marvellous crowd dispersed away,
The wise to weep, the thoughtless to be gay,
The young to wonder, and perhaps to sigh,
At this vain ending of mortality :
And I, a bard obscure, to ask of fame,
If this same trumpet-sounding of a name,
Blown through all ages with unfailing breath,
Is what mankind calls glory,—and if death,

Who seals the understanding and the eyes,
Of the shrunk worm that in his coffin lies,
Still leaves the ear, as in our mortal days,
Alive to censure or attuned to praise.
Again I took my solitary stand,
In a far hamlet of our western land,
As Summer in her greenest robe had drest.
The banks where Taw expands his silver breast;
Soft clime, where nature spreads with lavish hand,
Her brightest colours o'er the cultured land;
It was a churchyard where the branching yew,
O'er path and wall a sombre shadow threw,
And mound and stone preserved with sacred care,
The names and virtues of the sleepers there,
Save where oft-passing footsteps had effaced,
The fond device by love or friendship traced:
And on the grey and weather-beaten tower,
The clock still tolled the swift departing hour,
As when to other ears in olden times,
It pealed the measure of its dreamy chimes:
And there I saw, beside a grave new made,
A white-haired sexton leaning on his spade,
Some rustic idlers with inquiring look,
And village pastor with his open book:

A single mourner came, bowed down with grief,
Whose years had reached the changing of the leaf,
Life's autumn, when the flowers and fruits depart,
Storm-shaken from the seared and withered heart,
And the sad soul by many a care opprest,
Would flee away from hence and be at rest.
And he they buried had not reached the hour,
When youth attains its full meridian power,
His was the cruel inheritance of clay,
To pass in Spring's unripened bloom away.
And to my questioning, thus answered one,—
" She is a widow,—he, her only son :"
And I some honest tears could scarce refrain,
But then remembered how in ancient Nain,
A form appeared beside a lowly bier,
Speaking the words of comfort and good cheer,
Who though invisible is present still,
In all extremities of human ill ;
And thus are we through fiery ordeals brought,
By tribulation purified and taught,
Knowing that from this bondage we shall rise,
Plumed to ascend beyond these clouded skies ;
And that with high and low, and small and great,
We only share the universal fate,

Which makes, when this vain tragedy is past,
The drama's ending even at the last :
For Time at length to one estate shall bring,
The peer and peasant, cottager and king,
When disappear the demarcations wide,
Drawn by some orthodox pretence of pride,
And bones sectarian difference would divide,
May unmolesting slumber side by side,
Where the sharp conflict of existence o'er,
The strife of swords or pens disturb no more.
And haply, nurtured by their common mould,
The verdant turf will gentle flowers unfold,
Types of a passionless repose below,
And newer life which shall hereafter grow
Out of corruption, with immortal wings,
Fed by soft dews from heaven's eternal springs.

Son of the morning! of all stars most bright,
Cast headlong from the empyrean height,
When thy rebellious host were downwards hurled,
To bring contagion to an infant world ;
How wert thou fallen ! since first amidst the throng
Of angels mingled thine adoring song,

As the glad seraphs at creation's birth,
Gave joyous welcome to a new-made earth,
Ere vengeance thrust thee from thy home sublime,
To taint the bliss of Eden's golden prime !
Dread harbinger of evil ! in thy train,
Were war and famine, pestilence and pain,
And disobedience with attendant woe,
To mar God's glorious image here below,
And send him scared with sin's unfading brand,
To wring subsistence from the stubborn land,
And eat, in throb of brain and sweat of brow,
The hard-earned daily bread, as he does now !
Ah ! who can count the anguish and the fears,
Since Time first drank the tide of human tears ?
The oft repeated tale still fills each page,
Of his sad chronicle from age to age,
Oppression's chains and persecution's hate,
The scorn which merit suffers from the great,
Truth's champions exiled for their conscience' sake,
Or martyred at the scaffold or the stake,
And death at last, exultant over all,
The hearse, the winding-sheet, the funeral-pall ;
Ashes to ashes !——where remembering not
His grief, man sleeps, forgetting and forgot !

Yet think not Time, the triumph wholly thine!
Thou shalt not quench the living fire divine,
Which in the world's great warfare arms anew,
The languid soul with courage firm and true!
And wheresoe'er in life's unequal fight,
Undaunted virtue battles for the right,
Where outraged man in freedom's holy cause,
The threatening sword of retribution draws,
Or wakes to sense of contumely and wrong,
The cadence of imperishable song:
There, deathless, from the records of the past,
While this revolving universe shall last,
Their voices speak, to summon and to cheer,
The nations onward in their bright career,
Sounding from shore to shore, and sea to sea,
A clarion call to all who would be free.
Thus pealed on high the soul-awakening spell,
That winged with fatal aim the shaft of Tell,
That led, in Caledonia's hour of woe,
Her mustering clans to face the Saxon foe,
And yet incites the freeman's hand to wield,
Avenging arms on every blood-dyed field,
Where liberty, her long endurance o'er,
Invokes the brave to dare one struggle more.

And greater still, where gifted minds reveal,
The depths of science for the common weal,
Cleave the huge rock, or pierce the mountain side,
Or bridge the chasm deep, or river wide,
And forge the bonds that knit divided lands,
In one community of hearts and hands ;
Or blend the powers of loom, and press, and rail,
And commerce with her broad expanded sail,
And knowledge spreading far a holy calm,
O'er troubled states, a tranquilising balm,
Which bidding war depart and carnage cease,
Bind the glad world in one vast chain of peace.
Thus man throughout unmitigated ills,
Works out his own redemption and fulfils
His destiny predicted, and if aught
Be true, by seers foretold and prophets taught,
Then, in these latter days, through eyes of clay,
We hail the coming of the promised day :
Nor deem it but a visionary theme,
Or morbid wandering of a poet's dream,
If he, with fervent heart, and glance intent,
To scan the shadow of the near event,
Should haply, on some solitary steep,
Keep watch and ward while grosser natures sleep,

And thus proclaim from out his cloud-girt tower,
As slowly dawns the long-expected hour;
Sleepers, from ignominious slumber wake !
O'er yonder hills I see the morning break,
In the far east the first faint streaks of light,
Fringe the dim curtains of retreating night;
The powers of darkness flee this joyous earth,
And now enfranchised at a second birth,
Regenerate claim your heritage sublime,
Unscathed by sorrow, and untouched by Time !

REVISITING UMBERLEIGH BRIDGE,

NORTH DEVON.

ON REVISITING UMBERLEIGH BRIDGE, NORTH DEVON.

" And this our life exempt from public haunt,
    Finds tongues in trees, books in the running brooks,
    Sermons in stones, and good in everything."

SHAKESPEARE.

AGAIN, while Autumn's melancholy winds
Steal through the yellow woods, and scatter far
The withered glories of the waning year,
I stand midst Umberleigh's o'erhanging shades,
Where the antique bridge spans the winding Taw ;
All sights and sounds speak of autumnal days,
Of fields with plenty crowned, of harvest ripe,
Of summer gone, though yet her lingering green,
Blends with the russet tint of yonder copse,
Enough for memory to see and weep :
No mist obscures the thin clear atmosphere,
Through which the dead leaf noiseless falls to earth :
Nought breaks the deep repose of hill and dale,

Save the hoarse brawling of the turbulent stream,
While ever drearily the night wind sighs,
As if the spirits of the flood and field,
Gave a wild dirge to the departing year.
The very birds are mute, who late awoke,
In choral harmony, the listening groves,
Where the sad Dryad sees her sylvan shrine
Forsaken by the minstrels of the air,
Who faithless, like the false and fickle world,
Follow where Fortune smiles and sunbeams shine.
All the gay throng are fled, save one, who tunes
His plaintive melody on yonder spray,
The redbreast, come in dreary hours to cheer,
With his companionship, the walks of men.
Bird of the faithful heart! in weal or woe,
Thy constant song falls mournful on the ear;
So when December in his icy car,
Bids hospitality unfold her doors,
Thou at the hearth shalt be a welcome guest,
For this unbought, untutored melody.
Lifeless, and sad, and still, all nature seems;
While gliding on, the noble river flows,
As days, and years, and ages roll along,
Amidst perpetual change around, unchanged,

As when primeval Time first saw him pour,
In all the freshness of creation's birth,
Forth to the western main his glancing wave.

Chief of our northern streams, majestic Taw!
From thy clear fount on Dartmoor's rocky steep,
Where ancient legend marks the Druid's grave,
Thy limpid course is through sequestered vales,
And meadows broad, and glens, and sloping woods,
By Eggesford's wide demesne and Newnham's arch,
By Presbury's amphitheatre of hills,
And now enlarged by tributary brooks,
Thy waters flow by Brightley, where, of old,
In grey seclusion rose the monk's abode.
There, though the altar and the priest be gone,
Imagination brings their shadowy forms,
And hears monastic bells upon the wind.
And here, tradition says, the Saxon king*
Mourned o'er his country's wrongs, and nerved his arm,
To battle back the fierce adventurous Dane,
And sweep the proud oppressor from the land.
Spirit of patriotism! which from sire to son,

* Athelstane.

Unquenchable descended to this hour,
Behold! outnumbered by the savage foe,
The Saxon metal, calm and unsubdued,
As Britain, in the cause of injured man,
On Alma's bank and Inkermann's dread field,
Unfurls her standards to the gazing world,
Marching in freedom's van to victory!

Taw rushes on to reach his briny home,
And mingle with the far Atlantic wave,
Where Lundy's cliffs, unshaken by the storm,
Frown o'er the tumult of contending seas;
Upon his ruffled breast the crisp-brown leaves
Float like the faded joys of dreaming youth,
Borne on the current of destroying time,
And lost for evermore.
Ye oracles of earth, and sea, and sky,
Who in your varied aspects to the wise
Instruction bring, the thoughtless herd of men
Pass by, and note ye not!   For them, in vain
The universe displays her mystic book;
They taste no freshness in the dawn of Spring,
No gladness in the Summer's ardent breath,

No mournful pleasure on autumnal eves,
Nor awe, when Winter from the frozen north,
Unchains his blasts to sweep the prostrate globe :
Ambition, mammon, pleasure, lead them on,
In cities great, amidst the restless crowd
Of worldlings, seeking unsubstantial joys.
Hence false delights! give me this calm retreat,
Far from the rude realities of life,
Where I, beneath the spreading shade of oaks,
May listen to the fall of rivulets,
Or sound of sheep-bells on a mountain side,
Or cry of rooks, or catch the balmy scent
Of gathered hay-fields in luxuriant June,
When village chimes give to the trembling air,
The joyous note of rustic festival :
Or mark the fleecy and fantastic clouds,
That congregate upon the verge of day,
When Hesperus leads forth the starry hosts,
Countless, mysterious, everlasting lights,
To number whom 'twere vain ; so genius taught
By inspiration, how these glittering orbs
Are poised revolving in unmeasured space,
Thus marvelling cried : " In wisdom I am one,
Collecting fragments on a wondrous shore,

The confines of illimitable seas,
Whose mighty depths are unexplored beyond!"
Fountains of truth ! above, below, around,
Voiceless, but full of language eloquent,
Ye whisper to the soul, that earth thus clad
In her autumnal garb, midst falling leaves,
And forests bare, is but the type of man,
Fading into the winter of his days,
And never more to greet returning spring !
Yet shall the fields renew their vernal bloom,
Again the glowing landscape shall rejoice,
Once more the silver stream shall mirror back,
The many-coloured tints of April skies ;
Again the lark shall carol to the dawn,
When the young morning lifts her veil of clouds,
To walk in freshness o'er the purple hills ;
A thousand harmonies shall fill the air,
The balm of odorous plants, the busy hum
Of insects peopling the noontine ray,
Warmed into rapturous being, shall proclaim
The jubilee of an awakening world.
All shall revive, the germ of life remains
Warm in its sepulchre of wintry snow,
Foreshadowing to the philosophic muse,

A season when the disenfranchised mind,
Upspringing to its heritage of light,
Shall mingle with eternal things of day,
Like them immortal, changeless, unsubdued.

And now my pensive steps I homeward turn,
But deep engraven on my heart shall dwell
This pictured scene, and though to other climes
I journey forth, yet oft in fancy's dream
The soul shall wander back ; once more I'll tread
The margin of this deep and devious flood,
And mark the sunlight o'er its current play,
What time the harebell sheds her pendant bud,
On grassy slope and moss-embroidered dell.
The village inn, the ivy covered rock,
The decent cot amidst uncultured flowers,
The hawthorn blossom by the gentle stream,
The tottering bridge reared by forgotten hands,
Shall wake soft visions of departed days,
And fill the page which memory loves to keep,
Sacred to years when life and hope were young.

Farewell, sweet Umberleigh, a long farewell !
Oft shall the pilgrim turn when evening throws

Her lengthening shadows from the dreamy west,
To watch thy limpid waters ceaseless flow,
While midst descending dews, the tranquil night
Steals gently on, and to the weary mind,
As now to mine, communicates her peace.
Thou wilt be still the same, when he who gives
This ineffectual strain shall sing no more:
Again the wild rose shall thy banks adorn,
Thy woods be green, thy skies serene and clear,
Thy waters murmur o'er their pebbly bed,
Sparkling and swift beneath the summer beam,
Thy groves still clad in leafy pride of May,
For ever fragrant, and for ever fair!

Oct. 31, 1854.

TO SWEDEN.

"What Sweden wants is rather faith in the future, than pride in the past."—*Examiner*, November 21, 1855.

Arm Scandinavia! shall the Swede,
Shrink pale and spiritless afar,
When Freedom in her hour of need,
Calls her avenging sons to war,
Against the stern imperious Czar?

Sing not the lays of olden time,
O'er wassail bowls by glowing fires,
For worthless is the idle rhyme,
Unless the minstrel's voice inspires,
In sons the daring of their sires!

While kindling o'er the Norseman's fame,
Prophetic bards thy future scan,
Bid them to sounding harps proclaim,
That foremost for the rights of man,
Sweden triumphant leads the van!

Shall centuries of hate suppressed,
With threatened wrongs provoke no blow,
While rankles in each Swedish breast,
Remembrance of the savage foe,
Who at Pultowa laid ye low?

While floats his flag o'er Cronstadt's tower,
He wistful eyes the Baltic main,
And waits but some propitious hour,
To wrest from thee thy fair domain,
And rivet round thy neck the chain!

This is the day by seers foretold,
And watched by earnest hearts and eyes,
When Freedom midst her grief grown bold,
Thus to the startled nations cries:
"My hour is come—awake, arise!"

She scatters in her onward path,
Systems and creeds of priests and kings,
Treads down oppression in her wrath,
While o'er the troubled world she brings
Repose, with healing in her wings.

From Himalaya to the steep,
Of Andes' cloud-encircled height,
O'er isles that gem the western deep,
Her empire dawns, serene and bright,
And universal as the light.

She calls thee from thy pine-clad hills,
From mountain slope and forest deep,
By earth's accumulated ills,
Where despots crush and kingdoms weep,
To rouse indignant from thy sleep!

Leave time-worn trophies of the past,
'Tis thine the Avenger's blade to wield,
Thine must be now the trumpet's blast,
The march, the camp, the battle-field,
The sword, the banner, and the shield!

Arm Scandinavia! come ye brave,
Like billows on a wintry sea,
Leave doubt and fear to serf and slave,
Unworthy Liberty and thee,
Strike home, and be for ever free!

ROBERT BURNS.

A CENTENARY POEM.

ROBERT BURNS.

A CENTENARY POEM.

ONE OF THOSE HIGHLY COMMENDED BY THE JUDGES AT THE CRYSTAL PALACE COMPETITION.

> " Gie me ac spark o' Nature's fire,
>   That 's a' the learning I desire ;
>   Then tho' I drudge thro' dub an mire'
>   At plough or cart,
>   My Muse, though hamely in attire,
>   May touch the heart."—BURNS.

CLIME of rude hills and glens and moorlands bare,

Of heath-clad summits and of valleys fair,

Of winding river and o'erhanging wood,

Where frowns the forest and where foams the flood ;

Stern Caledonia ! thine a gifted throng

Of sons renowned in arms and skilled in song ;

Whether by Lucknow's walls they conquering sweep,

Or cleave with reckless prow the Arctic deep ;

Whether their breath the border slogan fills,

Or shepherd's pipe by Ettrick's sparkling rills,

Or court the Muse, or fearless tempt the gale,
Where busy commerce spreads the frequent sail ;
Thy fame they bear alike o'er sea and shore,
From Ganges' marge to frozen Labrador !

And thou ! sweet Poet of this mountain land,
Who touched her wild harp with the master's hand,
When Genius called thee from the peasant's toil,
To sing the glories of thy native soil ;
She marked thy glowing spirit heavenward stray,
Thy passion's strength, thy "pulse's maddening play,"
And bade thee paint, with truth-directed pen,
Old Scotland's scenes, her manners, and her men,
While verse divine thy weary task beguiled,
Chief of the northern Bards ! fair Nature's self-taught
      child !
Nurtured in tempests was thy humble birth,
As Spring unfolds to deck reviving earth,
When she through chill surrounding snows puts forth,
Some hardy offspring of the ice-clad north,
Some mountain flower fast rooted in the rock,
Proof to the storm king's wrath and whirlwind's
      shock ;

Like thee unmoved, midst howling blasts to grow,

Gathering fresh strength from all the winds that blow.

'Twas thine to roam in boyhood's marvelling hour,

By lonely dell, or grove, or haunted tower,

Or oft, by Fancy, led through meadows fair,

Where fragrant birks o'erspread the banks of Ayr ;

While from the rosy depth of summer sky,

Fell on thine ear the wild bird's melody,

The lavrock's carol to the brightening morn,

The plover's cry o'er distant moorland borne ;

Or, from the breezy slope of upland height,

While the sad gloaming led the tranquil night,

To mark the everlasting lights return,

Orion glisten, or Arcturus burn,

Voiceless to sordid worldlings, but to thee

Revealing in their silent mystery,

Such harmonies as through creation rang,

When all the sons of heaven together sang,

As the young planets and the sister stars,

Rolled through the universe their golden cars.

Or stretched by Lugar's stream or Irvine's side,

Or midst green shades to watch soft Logan glide,

And wrapt at meditation's pensive hour,

To yield the soul to thought's creative power,

Lulled by the distant and the dreamy fall
Of waters, mingling with the cushat's call;
Or when the gust, on melancholy eves,
Strewed thick and fast the sere autumnal leaves,
Or ruthless winter stripped the quivering tree,
And swept o'er frost-bound hills of Ochiltree,
Thy spirit walked with Nature, free to trace
Each varying form of grandeur and of grace,
And in her wide and universal book,
By hoary mount, or glen, or wandering brook,
To read all things sublime, and good, and fair,
And drink the fount of Inspiration there!
Nor there alone thy dawning muse had birth,
But in that home of unassuming worth,
Where, round "the wee bit ingle's" flickering light,
Love's sunshine cheered the long December's night,
Where dwelt, oft bred on Scotia's rugged soil,
The dignity of independent toil;
There—where the sterner virtues held control,
Did free-born thoughts possess thine ardent soul,
Found not where pensioned flattery crawling, brings
Obsequious homage to the thrones of kings.
Or charm'd by ballad old of minstrel grey,
That told of belted knight or border fray;

How leal Montrose the headman's axe defied,
To quench in blood the patriot's fiery pride ;
Or how with Highland chivalry arrayed,
Lochiel the gentle, bared the clansman's blade,
When Lowland steel laid chief and vassal low,
With brow erect, and face toward the foe.
And thy young breast with kindling ardour burned,
To hear how trampled man indignant turned,
As on the tyrant's crest avenging fell,
The sword of Wallace, and the shaft of Tell !
Then did thy fervent heart o'erburdened long,
Break forth in all the eloquence of song—
Thine was each measure, sad, or grave, or gay,
The soldier's war-cry, or the lover's lay,
Weaving one exquisite mysterious chain,
That links each absent Scot by mount and main,
And brings a shadowy band to mem'ry's shrine,
The dreams of youth, and days of " auld lang syne."
When far from Yarrow and the braes of Doon,
The exile hears each well-remembered tune,
His native hills and skies before him gleam,
The wood, the rock, the vale, the rushing stream,
And spell-bound by that soft enchanting strain,
He joyous treads Ben Lomond's heath again.

Come from the city and the court—vain throng!
And roam the sunny woodland depths among,
And breathe the balm of unpolluted air,
And hear the Poet's solemn teachings there ;
How throbs his heart with bliss unfelt by you,
As worshipping the Beautiful and True,
Apostle-like, in temples great he stands,
At altars pure, raised not by mortal hands !
And he is named Deliverer in the skies,
On earth a guardian angel in disguise,
Cheering the languid soul thro' paths of woe,
Though he must wear the crown of thorns below.
Spurn not his task ! he speaks of that glad time,
Foretold by seers and prophet-bards sublime,
When Freedom, armed with thunders loud and deep,
Shall rouse the prostrate nations from their sleep,
While at the muster of his war array,
Oppression's thrones shall crumble into clay.
Then shall the desert blossom as the rose,
Then shall be dried the fount of human woes,
While radiant Truth, descending earthward, brings
Love by his side, and healing in his wings,
Peace to the troubled shores of lands distrest,
Joy to the sad, and to the weary—rest.

Say, scornful world! where Dives fares in state,

While Lazarus starves and shivers at the gate,

Where Wealth, unheeding Penury's faint cry,

Rolls in his gilded chariot proudly by,

Where Mammon turns humanity to gold,

And youth grows grey, and famished childhood old;

Say! does the Poet lift his torch in vain,

Who clears the shadows from these tracks of pain,

Who draws from slumbers deep, at song's control,

Each finer impulse of the charmed soul,

Or bids soft Charity her solace bear,

Where threadbare Merit lingers in despair,

Pointing, to pallid Want's expiring eye,

That better land beyond this darkened sky?

Or calls the brave, when man oppresses man,

Fearless for Liberty to lead the van,

And wakes those mighty spirits which of yore,

At Bannockburn her flag defiant bore,

As rose from rank to rank the thrilling cry,

Forward, ye Scots! the word is, " Do or die?"

No! though obscure his lot who breathes the strain,

Too wise for Folly and her flaunting train,

Whose notes inspired, toil's darkening hours beguile,

Bidding forsaken grief look up and smile,

And hail amidst the storm that flashes by,
Man's heritage of Immortality :
Though his the broken heart and early doom,
Lit by the lamp of genius to the tomb,
Where flattery carves not on the sculptured stone,
A pompous list of virtues ne'er his own,
Yet, if his voice has stirred one holy thought,
In breast o'erladen, and in brain o'erwrought,
Or nerved one wavering mind with steadier might,
Who in life's battles struggles for the right,
Or taught one soul by chastening anguish riven,
To leave the issue and event to Heaven ;
For him no marble honours need we raise,
His monument shall be a People's praise,
At every hearth, in every household known,
His thoughts shall be familiar mottos grown,
A wealth of words, with wit and wisdom rife,
The common phrases of their daily life ;
And pilgrim feet from many lands shall tread
The turf which blooms in verdure o'er his head,
And tears from manhood's eyes shall fall unseen,
To keep his grave and his remembrance green.
Greater than mightiest conquerors, who wield
The fate of worlds on Slaughter's crimson field,

Is he, divinely taught, who thus subdues
All mortal passions by his gentle muse,
Winning, 'midst ceaseless cares, the grand renown,
The Poet's triumph and the Martyr's crown.

Immortal BURNS! Such destiny was thine,
Onward, unquailing, in thy work divine,
Thick closing round o'erwhelming troubles throng,
Yet to the last thy heart was full of song,
From the first cloud that o'er Life's morning rose,
In thy great mission, faithful to the close.
We, through the mist of long-departed years,
Behold thee crushed by dark foreboding fears,
Asking of unborn days, as Fame's reward,
Love for the Man, and honour for the Bard.
Have then thy wish! here in a kindred land,
Where Freedom dauntless guards the wave-washed
          strand,
Where Science gives, beneath this crystal dome,
The Arts a shelter, and the Muse a home,
We dedicate to thee this festal day,
This nation's gathering, and this minstrel's lay,
And in that bold and Anglo-Saxon tongue,
By Shakespeare warbled and by Milton sung,

We raise the mingled shout of loud acclaim,
And blend with theirs, immortally, thy name—
High priests of Poesy, whose strains sublime,
Outlive the ruins and the wrecks of Time!

BURNS' CENTENARY POEMS.

MONTROSE'S GATHERING.

A.D. 1644.

THERE 's a sound that is rousing the clans of the
    north,
From Tweed to the Pentlands, from Clyde to the
    Forth,
Through lowlands and highlands the tidings are
    known,
That traitors have threatened the altar and throne ;
And the leal and true-hearted together shall come,
At scream of the pibroch and roll of the drum,
And Scotland's young chivalry wake from repose,
To set up the standard and follow Montrose !

The shepherd has left on the mountain his flocks,
And the herdsman his cattle to roam 'midst the rocks,
And the ploughman in haste has forsaken his team,
And the fisher his boat by the loch and the stream ;

And the deer upon Ettrick in freedom may stray,
For the hounds are at home and the hunters away,
They are gone from the hills where the heather-bell
    grows,
To set up the standard and follow Montrose !

Glengarry is marching o'er muirland and glen,
Clanranald the valiant has mustered his men,
Lochiel has beheld the red signal afar,
And Keppoch has answered the summons to war ;
They gather from Appin, they haste from Glencoe,
As leaves in the forest when autumn winds blow,
As brooks when the spring-tide has melted the snows,
They rush to the banners of dauntless Montrose !

They arm for the king, and the church, and the law !
And woe to Argyle when the claymore they draw !
And woe to the Campbells, they sheath not the brand,
Till traitors and treason are swept from the land !
One foot in the stirrup, one hand on the rein,
But at parting a cup to the cause they will drain,
To faction confusion, and honour to those,
Who have set up the standard and follow Montrose !

Then onward they come in close order arrayed,
The laird and his vassal with target and blade,
And they sweep from the hills like the lightning-
    charged cloud,
When waves are upheaving and tempests are loud ;
And as mists from the mountain-top vanish away,
And shadows depart at the breaking of day,
So perish for ever our fear-stricken foes,
Before the royal banner and gallant Montrose !

THE ARCTIC VOYAGER.

"Only one white man seems to have been living when their
tribe arrived, and him it was too late to save. An Esquimaux
woman saw him die. 'He was large and strong,' she said;
'and sat on the sandy beach, his head resting on his hands, and
thus he died.'"—NARRATIVE OF THE HUDSON'S BAY COMPANY'S
EXPEDITION.

ALONE upon the desert strand,
　　Beneath the bitter Arctic sky,
The last of the devoted band,
　　Resigned, he lays him down to die.

Around him spreads the frozen main,
　　Chill falls the sleet, the rough winds blow,
And far as aching eye can strain,
　　The pathless wilderness of snow.

No friendly voice the silence cheers,
　　His faithful comrades, where are they?
They stiffen on their icy biers,
　　To wintry storms and wolves a prey.

Famished and wan, yet unsubdued,
  With saddened brow and thickening breath,
Amidst that dreary solitude,
  He is alone, alone with death.

And where, in that appalling hour,
  Wander his thoughts? They are again,
Wafted by memory's subtle power,
  Far o'er the blue Atlantic main;

Back to that well-remembered clime,
  Where oft beneath the yew tree's shade,
He listened to the church bells' chime,
  Or pensive mused, or careless strayed;

And saw the dream of coming life,
  In visions dim before him pass,
The toil, the triumph, and the strife,
  Darkly beheld, as through a glass;

Or tracing o'er each mouldering stone,
  The frail memorials of the past,
Thought that amidst this dust, his own
  Should mingle in repose at last.

But not for him a resting place,
　In that fair isle beyond the waves,
Where sleep the ashes of his race,
　Wrapt in the mould of kindred graves.

Up springs the prayer, down falls the tear,
　The soul throws off her bonds of clay,
Faith is triumphant over fear,
　And thus his spirit passed away.

Too late the marvelling Esquimaux,
　Has reached the solitary shore,
Where mute, and motionless, and low,
　The white man sleeps to wake no more;

He who was first to do and dare,
　All perils of the flood and field,
And famine-struck, and wan with care,
　Unconquered yet, the last to yield.

As when on glory's course he steered,
　Northward the wreck-devoted bark,
Nor treacherous floe, nor iceberg feared,
　Nor threatening wave, nor tempest dark.

To that bleak land of mist and gloom,
  Where sound of life is never heard,
Where fleeting summer sheds no bloom
  Of herb, or flower, or song of bird.

Where desolation reigns supreme,
  Throned on the glacier's silent height,
Where idly falls day's feeble beam,
  And half the circling year is night.

There, while the snowdrift sweeping by,
  Obscured the far and languid sun,
Forward ! was still their leader's cry,
  And faint not till your work be done !

For kindly hearts shall forward press
  To bring the oft-expected aid,
And cheer the desert's loneliness,
  With succour near, though long delayed !

By rifted rock, by lonely isle,
  O'er dreary wastes, and mountains bare,
While stars above them coldly smile,
  They wander on in their despair.

Through years of suffering calmly borne,
  Still trusting on from day to day,
But graver each succeeding morn,
  As one by one their hopes decay.

Camped by the wild o'erhanging steep,
  Or barren shore of frost-bound lake,
They start from their unsheltered sleep,
  To watch the dull light slowly break.

Or mark the sea-fowl plume her flight,
  Safe through the trackless fields of air,
Unerring, though beyond her sight,
  To climes more genial, plains more fair.

And as her dim receding form,
  Fast lessens in the glimmering west,
They long like her from gathering storm,
  To flee away and be at rest.

Blest thought! for in her wild career,
  The hand that guides her course aright,
Unseen, unfelt, yet ever near,
  Can change their darkness into light.

To-morrow shall their griefs repay,
    Though o'er them keen the tempest raves,
Wait but the dawning of the day !
    To-morrow dawns, but on their graves.

They perished nobly, not in vain,
    They dared with constant hearts and bold,
The terrors of the frigid main,
    The whirlwind's wrath, the winter's cold.

And Bellot ! o'er thy bright career,*
    Untimely quenched beneath the wave,
From many lands shall flow the tear,
    For one so gentle, wise, and brave.

In brotherhood ye stand as one,
    And bards who wreaths of song entwine,
For deeds of worth and honour done,
    Shall weeping intermingle thine !

For thy true heart by zeal impelled,
    And kindred sympathy elate,
Its onward course unwavering held,
    To share their glory and their fate !

    * Lieutenant Bellot of the French Navy.

What though for them no marble shrine,
   Carved by the sculptor's hand be found,
Or chiselled by his art divine,
   A tomb on consecrated ground!

Nor wrapt in winding sheet nor shroud,
   Unblest their whitening bones decay,
While rude winds sing their requiem loud,
   By headland bleak and ice-bound bay!

Theirs the imperishable name,
   That as a meteor gleams afar,
An immortality of fame,
   Beyond the beam of polar star!

And duty, when on danger's track,
   She bids the brave her call pursue,
Dauntless and firm, not turning back,
   Though death be there, resolved and true,
One glorious end, one aim in view,
Shall point to Franklin and his crew!

                    May 31st, 1855.

ORIANA.

YE stars! for brighter things make room,
　Waste not your lustre on the night,
Since she is come to chase our gloom,
　Whose presence is perpetual light.

Ye blossoms of the earliest year,
　Who blow where first the wild birds sing,
We need ye not while she is here,
　Whose aspect is unchanging spring!

Where'er she moves, such grace appears,
　Whene'er she speaks, such accents fall,
As win to smiles or melt to tears,
　And hold our hearts in captive thrall.

And would ye know, whom all declare,
  In person, mind, and manners blest?
Go seek the fairest of the fair,
  In this famed region of the West!

'Tis she, of soul and look serene,
  Who mingling with the grave or gay,
Pursues with gentle voice and mien,
  Guileless, her unobtrusive way.

Love round her steps shall never cease,
  Each heaven-born gift and charm to pour,
And in her breast celestial peace,
  Unmoved shall dwell for evermore!

LUCKNOW.

On Lucknow's rampart stern arrayed,
We grasped, each man his battle blade,
Bereft of hope, but undismayed.

A traitor host around us lay,
Like tigers crouching for their prey,
And ten to one at least were they.

We looked, as did become the brave,
To Heaven omnipotent to save,
But dreaded not the soldier's grave.

Beneath those banners firm we stood,
That have sustained midst fire and blood,
Our country's name by field and flood.

The wail of women rent the air,
And in their weakness and despair,
The voice of children rose in prayer.

They were as those who stand in gloom,
Within the portals of the tomb,
Torture, and worse than death, their doom.

We swore that ere the savage foe,
Should ruthless lay those loved ones low,
In mercy we would strike the blow ;

And from polluting hands to save,
Take, Roman like, the life we gave,
And lay them stainless in the grave.

On rushed the fiends with many a yell,
And fast and furious o'er us fell,
The mingled crash of shot and shell;

But dauntless still our ground we held,
The rebel crew by rage impelled,
Assailing oft, yet oft repelled.

Next morn with terror would be rife,
The last of suffering and strife,
The last of liberty and life.

We yield to fate, but not to fear,
We fall where duty bids us,—here,
These blackened walls shall be our bier ;

Bequeathing as the Spartan band,
A beacon light to every land,
Where valour makes his final stand.

But hark ! what music shrill and clear,
Familiar to the Highland ear,
Breaks through the clash of sword and spear !

'Tis but the wind, or wild bird's scream,
Lending a momentary gleam,
To brighten hope's expiring dream.

It is no dream, that piercing strain
Sounds o'er the din of arms again,
And shadows gather on the plain ;

The flash of bayonets glistened then,
And now is heard from yonder glen
The measured tramp of armèd men.

It is Macgregor's battle cry,
His slogan screams from earth to sky,
The long-expected succour's nigh !

With claymore broad, and bonnet blue,
They come, the loyal and the true,
To save the faithful and the few !

They sweep like eagles on their prey,
Fierce in the foray or the fray,
Death and destruction mark their way !

Soon shall the treacherous foeman feel,
The clansman's keen avenging steel,
And backward in confusion reel.

And nearer yet that pibroch fills
The air, as oft on Scotland's hills,
It's martial note the listener thrills.

Blest be that note, and blest the power,
Bringing as sunshine thro' the shower,
Deliverance in such an hour!

Snatched from the burning like a brand,
Or wreck from off a rocky strand,
Or bird from out the fowler's hand.

This deed shall many a bard recall,
Around the hearth at evening's fall,
In lowly hut and lordly hall;

When yule logs cheer the wintry night,
And wine cups sparkle in the light,
Where festal fires are burning bright.

And England's heart with pride shall beat,
For sons who never know defeat,
When nations in the conflict meet.

Who build in Freedom's name a fane,
By many a river, rock, and plain,
From Indus to the Arctic main.

And thus uphold in every clime,
Untarnished by the rust of time,
Her glory, peerless and sublime!

January, 1858.

POETS OF THE PEOPLE.

POETS OF THE PEOPLE.

GERALD MASSEY.

MINSTREL of Hope! whose care-consoling song,
   Lights up the gloom where labour works and weeps,
Thy master hand with impulse soft or strong,
   The chords of grief or joy alternate sweeps;
By grave of buried love we hear thy dirge,
   And vainly would the ready tear restrain,
Or start, as swells the storm awakened surge,
   When wintry tempests vex the sleepless main,
     Roused by the clarion call that fills thy battle
       strain!

Yet ever trustful that the coming time,
   Shall dawn in gladness o'er this weeping earth,
And change, as sung by prophet bards sublime,
   Night into day, and mourning into mirth:

When Freedom, like a giant armed for strife,
  With sword unsheathed and banner red unfurled,
Shall lift the slumbering nations into life,
  And bid oppression from his thrones be hurled,
  While mercy reigns benign, and love subdues the
    world!

CAPERN.

BARD of the stream, the greenwood and the glen,
  Led by thy lay, I quit the busy throng,
Of populous cities and the haunts of men,
  To wander musingly the fields among,
And breathe the fragrance of awakening spring;
  I feel the breeze upon my pale cheek blow,
I hear the lark his matin blithely sing,
  While at my feet fresh waters murmuring flow,
  And flowers are blooming fresh, and winds are
    whispering low !

Sing on ! and teach the vain and sordid crowd,
  Bending to gilded idols of the hour,
Where folly holds her revels long and loud,
  That in the poet's soul there is a power,

Beyond the reach of fashion or of fate,

    Or pride of birth, or broad ancestral lands,

Since he inspired does his own joy create,

    As worshipping the Beautiful, he stands

    In temples great and fair, built not by mortal

        hands.

CARRINGTON.

His spirit loved our desolate Dartmoor hills,
　　The silent and unpeopled solitude ;
The giant tors, wild wastes, and rushing rills,
　　Where neither voice nor foot of man intrude ;
There, fashioned by an unseen influence,
　　He did attune so sweet and true a strain,
That the charmed river-god who joyous thence,
　　Pours out his brooks to swell the western main,
　　Leant listening on his urn to catch the notes again.

And Tamar still bounds sparkling on his way,
　　And heath flowers crown the fairy-haunted steep,
The wild bird warbles where by cromlech grey,
　　The Druid and his mystic worship sleep ;
Thus, though the poet's heart and hand be cold,
　　We hear his voice the woods and streams among,
Nature's eternal poetry as of old,
　　Still through the gathering ages doth prolong,
　　The harmony divine of his perpetual song.

MEN OF THE PEOPLE.

MEN OF THE PEOPLE.

GEORGE STEPHENSON.

No lineage claimed he from the titled great,
No rich inheritance of lands or gold,
His lot was cast in ordinary mould,
To wrestle with the purposes of fate,
And from his cold obscurity to rise,
By force of an unconquerable will,
And soul defiant of extremes of ill,
A marvel unto men's astounded eyes;
He did the turbulent elements constrain
To gentle servitude, and could subdue
By skill their wondrous strength, until it grew
Obedient as a steed beneath the rein.
Mind conquering matter! an achievement stored
With nobler triumphs than the battle field,
Since he has taught the coming age to wield,
A power more potent than the brandished sword,

Which binding shore to shore and clime to clime,
Shall bring the advent of that promised time,
When war with silent trump and banners furled,
Shall vanish from a new awakened world.

SIR JOHN FRANKLIN.

FAR from the genial isle that gave him birth,
In the dread region of eternal cold,
Where winter and primeval darkness hold,
In icy fetters, ocean, air, and earth ;
Where life has reached its limit, and the glow
Of the returning sun revives no more,
His ashes rest on some untrodden shore,
His dirge the wail of winds, his shroud the snow ;
Thither at duty's summons prompt he came,
With heart intrepid and devotion true,
Nor doubt, nor fear of death, nor danger knew,
Nor aught save glory and his country's name.
This tale by poets told, shall waken tears,
And bring fresh colour to the cheek of age,
And rouse our youth all perils to engage,
When England calls them in her future years ;
And they in native daring shall arise,
Winning renown for noble enterprise,
Unceasing, as the glistening spheres that roll,
For ever round the ice-encircled pole.

GARIBALDI.

WARRIOR and statesman! In her hour of need,
Writhing beneath oppression's iron tread,
Thy country bids thee lift her from the dead,
That she, long suffering, be from bondage freed.
Land of the bards and heroes! mighty men,
Famous in arms and unsurpassed in song,
We blend the glories that to thee belong,
With Rafaelle's pencil and with Petrarch's pen !
And now the spirit of thine ancient might
Is wakened, and with ruthless grasp shall shake
The double-headed eagle on his throne, and make
Just laws and pure, and wrong shall yield to right ;
And subtle creeds and false philosophies,
Woven by priestcraft on Rome's seven hills,
Shall melt like shadows when the morning fills,
With universal light all earth and skies.
Then shall be heard from Alps to Apennines,
Loud as the wind that rends the giant pines,
When storms are mightiest on the sleepless sea,
A voice proclaiming—Italy is free !

Nov. 26th, 1859.

THE SKYLARK'S PETITION.

Suggested by an incident in a London police court, where the presiding magistrate, Mr. Yardley, interceded for the liberation of a skylark.

Let me again be free,
That I may speed away o'er meadows fair,
And carol as I cleave the cloudless air,
    My full heart's melody !

For I, a songster born,
Would shake the dews of morning off my wing,
And from my mossy bed exulting spring,
    Where waves the yellow corn.

Not in the pent-up street,
Can your caged captive wake the joyous song,
Nor midst the ceaseless strife of men, where throng
    Loud tongues and restless feet.

Mine was the mountain breeze,
On fern clad hills, where purple harebells grow,
And silver brooks make music as they flow,
    Beneath the forest trees.

There was my place of rest,
Whence upon fluttering pinions upward borne,
I hailed the crimson streaks of coming morn,
    Warm from my grassy nest.

Ere the white mists were curled,
Back from the lonely peak of mountain grey,
In the far clouds was heard my matin lay,
    While slept the silent world.

The ploughman knew my voice,
Driving his team along the furrowed soil,
The sun-burnt reaper paused amidst his toil,
    To listen and rejoice.

No notes of mine have birth,
Save in the depths of yonder summer sky,
When stars grow dim and murky shadows fly,
    From the awakening earth.

Unbar my prison door,
That poised on tremulous and outstretched plume.
Or soaring heavenward, I may resume
My minstrel art once more!

For He that fashioned thee,
Gave to my slender throat the power of song,
He made us both, the feeble and the strong,
But made all creatures free!

IN MEMORIAM.

BRUNEL.

OBIIT. SEPT. 15, 1859.

> " He shall not welter to the parching wind
>   Without the meed of one melodious tear."
>
> LYCIDAS.

INEXORABLE Time !   Sweeping away
The great and gifted, and the good and wise!
As falls thy noiseless foot from day to day,
Fast fade from sight the forms we mostly prize ;
Into the shadows of the silent land
Swiftly they glide ; nor can we count them o'er,
So thick they congregate upon the strand
Of that mysterious sea, from whose dark shore
Vainly we call them back,—they will return no more.

Thus stand we round his grave who yesternight,
In the completeness of his wide renown,
Had scaled on Glory's track the topmost height,
To win from her a world-approvèd crown ;

But genius has her martyrs, and opprest
In the stern conflict, in the strife of mind,
Now wearily he lays him down to rest,
And all of mortal man he leaves behind,
Is one poor heap of dust, this morn to dust consigned.

Yet his the triumph—with the Titan race
Of mighty spirits who for earth have wrought
More glories than her kings, he takes his place,
Immortalized amidst the sons of thought ;
The fire that warmed his breast through anxious days
Of patient toil, still burns a quenchless flame,
A beacon light to young ambition's gaze,
And one more constellation finds a name,
Amongst the countless stars that fill the heaven of fame.

No record needs he on cathedral walls
To chronicle his deeds, no gilded tomb,
Where tenderly the softened daylight falls
On shrines of saints and heroes wrapt in gloom ;
Nor lay of bard, who thus with unskilled hand,
Would scatter o'er his urn the flowers of song ;
Upon the mountains of his native land
Are his achievements writ, to her belong
The proud memorials that around his footprints throng.

And England in her conquests yet to come,
Her marvellous future—bidding discord cease,
Not clad in arms, at beat of hostile drum,
Leading the nations in the chains of peace;
When she has multiplied the links that bind,
From Himalaya to the setting sun,
In one vast brotherhood all human kind,
And sees exulting 'midst the victories won,
Her noblest task fulfilled, her holiest mission done;

Then wheresoe'er by river, rock, or plain,
Subduing nature for the weal of man,
He taught her giant ships to plough the main,
Or reared the lofty arch of wondrous span;
There shall she claim for him a monument,
Greater than all the pyramids, nor less
Than classic fanes, since there the arts have lent
Their mingled powers the severed lands to bless,
And speed the onward course of mortal happiness.

STEPHENSON.

OBIIT. OCT. 12, 1859.

" Weep no more, woeful shepherds, weep no more,
  For Lycidas your sorrow is not dead."
                         LYCIDAS.

ONCE more! ere yet the echoes of our grief
Melt into air; before the tears are dry
Shed o'er departed worth, the circle brief
Of this autumnal moon scarce hastens by,
When the destroying angel smites again,—
One in the prime of honourable days,
Rich in esteem of all his fellow men,
In the full noon of reputation's blaze,
With love and reverence known in life's familiar ways.

Twin giant of his brother, gone before,
He too has dared, Prometheus-like, to climb,
The difficult steeps of knowledge to explore,
And build a name beyond the touch of time;

And science in his track with fostering care,
And peace their blessings manifold shall bring,
Plenty with golden horn, and commerce fair,
While freedom o'er the tranquil lands shall fling,
Watchful, the shadow broad of her protecting wing.

His task has lessened labour, vanquish'd space,
And through remotest years beheld afar,
His spirit leaves her everlasting trace,
Where'er impetuous speeds the fiery car;
And with his strength were childlike gentleness,
And tender sympathy, and prompt desire
To lift the fallen, with kindly words to bless,
And from his store of wisdom to inspire,
In youth's desponding breast, hope's reawakened fire.

Worthy his sire's renown, o'er whose young morn,
Cold penury her wintry shadows threw,
Alone in toil, in contumely, and scorn,
Still to his Heaven-appointed mission true;
For Nature on his soul the seal had set
Of her nobility—his high-wrought aim,
Stedfast through doubts, through wrongs devoted yet,
He wins at length amidst the world's acclaim,
And stands victorious on majestic hills of fame.

And in our island history enrolled,
Henceforth they are amongst the glorious dead,
The mighty unforgotten men of old,
Bards who have sung, and freemen who have bled :
O'er desert wastes parched by the tropic glow,
Fearless still following duty's clarion call,
Or locked in icy grasp of Arctic snow,
No dread could shake, no danger could appal,
The stern undaunted mind that triumphs over all.

They are not dead, but sleeping : from the past
Their voices speak,—and age shall teach to youth
The story of their lives ; conquerors at last,
Through calm endurance and heroic truth ;
As lamps upon some sea-surrounded tower
O'er the wild billows pour unchanging light,
So pressing onwards in the dark'ning hour,
We hail them, star-crown'd, on the eternal height,
Guiding through storm and strife, our faltering steps
    aright.

LAYS OF THE MONTHS.

H

LAYS OF THE MONTHS.

—

JANUARY.

FIRST born of months ! we greet thee with the chime
Of midnight bells from steeple and from tower,
As the dead year at his appointed hour,
Sinks in the void of all-devouring time :
Thou comest ! fur clad, from the northern seas,
The waters wide are frozen at thy breath,
All earth is shrouded in the garb of death,
And birds are silent on the leafless trees ;
Save one, in joy or grief—who singeth ever—
The redbreast, changeless minstrel, loved of old,
Whose heart grows warmer as the days wax cold,
With strain of cheerfulness that faileth never ;
And thick the snow flakes fall on mount and moor,
White as the page of life's unwritten book,
Whereon in thought profound the gazers look,
And marvel what the future has in store ;

Yet know we, from beneath her robe of sadness,

The world shall wake anew with songs of gladness,

And thus, though wintry storms are round us glancing,

We muster courage for the days advancing.

FEBRUARY.

THE rivulets are loosened from their chains,
There is a murmur of returning life,
Heard feebly 'midst the elemental strife
Of tempests lingering yet upon our plains ;
The golden crocus struggling through the snow,
And meek-eyed daisy, hardy mountaineer,
Greet us with salutation of good cheer,
Though pitiless above the keen winds blow ;
And ever and anon some songster tries,
The fragment of a half-forgotten strain,
Which he would carol to the woods again,
But for the chill breath of inclement skies ;
Thus o'er the broad and reawakening earth,
In herb, and bud, and lowly weed we see,
The types and shadows of mortality,
Bursting from sleep into a second birth ;
And more, we learn when hearts with grief are weary.
And sore the toil, and dark the path and dreary,
There is a power whose constant care can waken,
Light in his breast who walks with trust unshaken.

MARCH.

WAR clad, on pinions of the wind he leads
His boisterous legions through the troubled air,
Strewing with wrecks the seas, while forests bare,
Beneath his footsteps bend as shaken reeds ;
He stirs with his sharp breath our northern blood,
Waking the daring hardihood which bore
The Norseman bold from Scandinavia's shore,
To rule the land and subjugate the flood ;
He clears the vapours from our misty isles,
Gathering into the clouds a liquid store
Of dews, which o'er the thirsty lands shall pour,
Till the parched wilderness with verdure smiles ;
And so the teachings of adversity
Nerve the young soul with courage stern and true,
Which neither fate, nor change, nor chance subdue,
Though fierce Euroclydon be thundering by ;
And thus the mind from daily cares and sorrows,
A newer strength and clearer lustre borrows,
While she well armed, her upraised standard bearing,
Moves onward in her course, nor knows despairing.

APRIL.

SPRING wakes the woods, she comes in queenly state,
Her herald is that wandering bird whose strain,
The truant schoolboy loitering in the lane,
Loves with dissembling note to imitate ;
And o'er her ever-changing aspect gleam,
Fast fleeting shadow and alternate light,
Now dark with cloud and now with sunshine bright,
She fills with life, the hill, the vale, the stream :
And from above the rain drops shall descend,
And earth shall drink them deeply, and diffuse
Through leaf and flower all heaven's transcendant hues,
Till land and sky in glad communion blend.
Nothing in nature perisheth : the seed
Borne by the wind takes root again to bloom ;
Our death is but a slumber in the tomb,
To reappear from cold corruption freed :
And he who by the grave of vanished years,
Pours forth the tide of unavailing tears,
May consolation take and cease his weeping,
The buried treasure is not dead but sleeping.

MAY.

THERE is a melody of bird and bee,
All living things rejoice, the air with balm
Of plants grows fragrant, and a cloudless calm
Broods o'er the tranquil shore and shining sea;
The spirit of the universe awakes,
Earth gladdened at the spring's inspiring call,
From mountain blue, and wood, and waterfall,
Now with her thousand voices answer makes;
And hope and love go forth at dawn of day,
Where violets lurk in hazel copse unseen,
To gather blossoms white and garlands green,
And weave fresh roses for the queen of May.
Stay genial hours! ere yet the hand of pain,
Has traced on manhood's brow the lines of grief,
Ye speed too fleetly on your mission brief,
And visit not the saddened heart again!
Stay yet awhile, your rapid flight pursuing,
Care finds no balm since youth has no renewing,
Alas for Time, who will not brook delaying,
Though all the world be full of mirth and Maying!

JUNE.

'Tis sweet beneath this greenwood's quiet shade,
Rich in the foliage of the ripening year,
Far from the noise of towns to rest and hear
The soothing sound by falling waters made;
While from the meadows fresh, the new-mown hay
Blends with the perfume of the scented bean,
And through o'erarching elms is dimly seen
The village church with antique walls of grey:
The gay kingfisher spreads his painted wing,
The trout darts from his cover in the stream,
The skylark warbles to the morning beam,
Yet learnt he not in schools of art to sing.
All nature's works instruct the poet's eyes,
Who in creation's lowliest forms can see
The power and presence of Divinity,
Prompting the soul to muse and moralize;
And from the dreamland of his rest awaking,
With words of fire the startled silence breaking,
He gives the visions of his charmèd slumbers,
Enduring shapes in song's immortal numbers.

JULY.

GORGEOUS she comes, as orient queen of old,
In robe of Tyrian dye, whose syren smile
The conqueror of nations did beguile,
And Rome's stern chief in silken thraldom hold :
In glens and glades she has her sylvan court,
By brooklets clear where branching cedars wave,
And nymphs who haunt the fountain and the cave,
Around her throne in mirthful measure sport ;
The Dryads hear her voice, with nimble feet
Satyr and Faun keep rural revelry,
And tuneful Pan beneath the beechen tree,
Fills the still woodland with his fluting sweet.
Thus sang the masters of the classic lyre,
Weaving the mysteries they could not see,
Into one dream of glorious Poesy—
They sought, but found not the Promethean fire.
Their deities are dust, and naught remains,
Saving the deathless music of their strains,
Yet not in vain they touched with spirit strong,
And skilful hand the silver chords of song.

AUGUST.

I LOVE to climb the hills at sunset's glow,
Cooled by the soft breath of the western wind,
And listless on the grassy turf reclined,
To watch the pictured landscape far below ;
The shining river gliding glad and free,
By stately parks, and farms, and cottage homes,
The distant city with her spires and domes,
And far beyond, the blue eternal sea.
It is the summer's prime ; forest and plain
Are clothed with deeper hues, the cultured field
Gives promise that the teeming land shall yield,
In her due season stores of golden grain :
So in the noontide glory of our years,
We gain the summit of life's pilgrimage ;
Behind us youth, before us care and age,
A dim futurity, perchance of tears ;
Yet growing old and grey and coldly wise,
We cast aside some crude asperities,
And sage experience gives to manhood's eye,
The temperate glance of calm philosophy.

SEPTEMBER.

In garb of russet brown, the sober year
Sits like a matron, pensive, calm, and grey,
The glowing tints of youth have passed away,
And all her blossoms faded, pale, and sere :
Yet there are sounds of gladness far and wide,
The mingled harmony of hound and horn
Awake the slumbering echoes of the morn,
And rouse the moorcock from the mountain side :
And sunburnt labour in the yellow fields,
His sickle flashing in the autumn sun,
Rejoices when his harvest work is done,
That grateful earth her mellow treasure yields :
So he, who when the spring put forth her leaves,
Drove deep his plough into the stubborn soil,
Now gathers fruitage of his patient toil,
Standing exultant 'midst the full-eared sheaves ;
And ye, who listen to this lay, take heed !
And clearing from your hearts each idle weed,
The seed ye sow with watchful culture keeping,
Shall fill your garners in the day of reaping.

OCTOBER.

A HOLY stillness reigns through earth and sky,
And dying tints upon the woods are spread,
So manifold, of purple green and red,
That they the painter's mimic art defy;
The leaves are beautiful in their decay,
And in the eye of contemplation seem
Lit by a second summer's transient beam,
Ere falling, they are trodden into clay.
Nature's deep voice is mute; she waits her doom,
Serene amidst the ashes of the past,
And on each feature lingers to the last,
The hectic flush of life's expiring bloom :
So, severing from the ties that bind us here,
Things through the mortal sight obscurely known,
And darkly seen, are more apparent grown,
In the soul's vision spiritually clear :
And on the inner man there falls a beam,
As starlight on some clear and tranquil stream,
Reflecting in the speechless sufferer's breast,
The cloudless heaven of his approaching rest.

NOVEMBER.

Joy has departed, and the year is dead,
Hither and thither by the tempest blown,
Her withered trophies in our path are strown,
And many a summer bird has southward fled.
So waits a fawning world on prosperous times,
And so, when dark the hours, and few the friends,
When keen adversity's chill rain descends,
They speed like swallows to more genial climes.
Blow, blow ye gales ! the maddened ocean stir,
Scaring the sea-fowl from her lonely rock,
Ye are no flatterers, when your ruthless shock
Drives to his doom the wave-worn mariner !
Fall, fall sad leaf! your voice dissembles not,
As slowly perishing from branch and spray,
With silent eloquence ye seem to say,
That thine and ours is but the common lot !
That time upon his course is ever speeding,
Regrets, and sighs, and tears, alike unheeding,
That manhood's fires grow dim and cease their burning,
That hope has taken wing, no more returning !

DECEMBER.

Now twine with ivy and the mistletoe,
And berries from the glistening holly tree,
A crown for ancient hospitality,
Who at our hearths bids festal wine cups flow ;
And in the spirit of that strain sublime,
Breathing to man goodwill, and love, and peace,
We pledge to all the world, of joy increase,
And concord, as befits this Christmas time ;
And though the snow-drifts gather at our doors,
And icicles are on the old mill wheel,
And hills are frost-bound, and the brooks congeal,
And the fierce north his arrowy sleet outpours,
Yet welcome wassail and the nut-brown bowl,
Wherewith our fathers in the days of old,
Circling the faggot's blaze, defied the cold,
To freeze the generous impulse of the soul !
And so our hearts, though winter's breath be keen,
Shall bloom with verdure like the holly green,
Kindling, as does the yule log's ruddy glow,
A warmth to thaw this bleak December's snow.

TO A YOUNG LADY WITH A MINUTE GLASS.

ON HER BIRTHDAY.

WHILE envious Time his circling course repeating,
　Proclaims the dawning of this festal day,
He whispers low with many a joyous greeting,
　That one more year of life has passed away.

Rejoice! while yet in youth's unclouded morning,
　You cull the fragrant flowers unstained by tears,
But not unheeded be this kindly warning,
　That cares must gather in advancing years!

Fain would I teach, but not to mar the gladness,
　Nor shroud the rainbow hues that o'er thee gleam,
Nor interweave one sombre thread of sadness,
　With the bright tints of hope's expectant dream.

Then let the gentle voice of wisdom guide thee,
 Behold! the sands are gliding through the glass,
Learn from the silent monitor beside thee,
 To catch the priceless moments as they pass!

So every day, and hour, and minute number,
 For noble ends, high thoughts, and virtue pure,
The present is thine own; awake from slumber!
 Who wins the fight must labour and endure.

Then shall thy spirit full of firm endeavour,
 Armed for the truth, triumphant warfare wage,
And thine shall be the wreath unfading ever,
 Which crowns with glory's light the brow of age.

And higher yet, above this world's dominion, .
 Aspiring seek the life that is to be,
When hoary Time shall fold his weary pinion,
 Lost in the dawn of Immortality!

BY THE WATERS OF BABYLON.

When fond remembrance bade us dream
   Of Zion and her lofty towers,
We sat by Babel's rolling stream,
   And wept away the lingering hours.

Our silent harps with chords unstrung,
   In the mute anguish of despair,
On drooping willow trees we hung,
   Which mourned o'er falling waters there.

Chaldea's chieftains stand around,
   With helm, and spear, and glittering brand,
They bid us sing with mirthful sound,
   The anthems of our Fatherland.

With lips that move, but hearts that break,
   In cold and stern captivity,
Say, can the fettered soul awake,
   The lays of freedom and the free?

No! should sad memory treacherous prove,
　　Jerusalem! in this hour of woe,
Should grief, or chains, or death remove,
　　From thee one thought, one tear we owe;

For ever hushed the tongue shall sleep,
　　That wakes in raptured melody,
Or minstrel hands that faithless sweep,
　　The strings in praise of aught save thee!

Remember Lord! that ruthless day,
　　When over Salem's prostrate wall,
Fierce Edom led his war array,
　　Exultant at the trumpet's call.

When flushed with pride of conquest gained,
　　The foeman's footstep scornful trod,
And heathen voice and hand profaned
　　The altars of the living God!

Arise! the bonds of Israel break!
　　On Babel's towers thy wrath outpour,
That in her marble halls shall wake
　　The sounds of revelry no more!

Before thy lightnings, let her shrines—
   Palace, and mart, and dome decay,
As when the rising day star shines,
   The mists of morning melt away!

Gather thine exiled sons again,
   From every land, and isle, and shore,
To blest Judæa's flowery plain,
   The remnant of the tribes restore!

WRITTEN IN SEVERE ILLNESS.

WEARY and sad upon this couch of pain,
A lonely watcher 'midst the waste of night,
I ask the solace of repose in vain,
And chide the tardy dawning of the light;
While o'er my vision pass in solemn gloom,
The shadows of the days that are no more,
Speaking like voices from the silent tomb,
Of hopes decayed, and joyous friends of yore,
Swept by the waves of time from life's eventful shore.

And more, remembrance does to me unfold,
All I have left undone of duty's part,
How unfulfilled the high resolves of old,
How full of weeds this unproductive heart!
And I resemble one who stands alone,
Amidst the reapers on an autumn morn,
Seeking to bind the sheaves in spring-time sown,
But finds, instead of fields of waving corn,
The harvest of remorse, the thistle and the thorn.

Restore blest health, my manhood's languid prime!

While o'er the misspent past I hopeless grieve,

So will I snatch this fleeting gift of Time,

And moments lost by heedless thought retrieve;

Again the feeble fires of life renew,

That I may yet with resolution keen,

And purpose firm the nobler path pursue,

To keep with deeds of worth my memory green,

Ere I depart from hence and be no longer seen!

PATIENCE IN TRIBULATION.

"——Flagrantior æquo"
" Non debet dolor esse viri, nec vulnere major."

Juvenal., Sat. 13.

GREAT minds in darkest grief their powers display,
Unknown in joy, as stars unseen by day;
Crushed flowers are sweetest; Virtue's dauntless breast,
Triumphs the most, when most by care oppressed;
The soul's nobility no king can make,
No fortune heighten and no sorrow shake;
She, amidst change and chance divinely bright,
Glows like the diamond with a constant light,
Which grind to dust, or shatter as you will,
The smallest fragment is a diamond still.

MOMENTOUS QUESTIONS.

WHEN Fate's unsparing hand shall break
The fragile thread that holds us here,
Say, shall the trembling spirit take
Her flight to some less sinful sphere?
Where cares that rend the mortal breast,
And days of toil and nights of pain,
And all this lower world's unrest,
Vex not the sleepless soul again?

And in that clime, where'er it be,
Amidst the stars that nightly glow,
Will she from human passions free,
Forget the forms she loved below?
Or will the strength of earthly ties,
Survive the dust she leaves behind,
And still attract from yonder skies,
The changeless and eternal mind?

Or is this death we cannot shun,
Total oblivion ? Will the spark
That lights us till our work be done,
Burn out, and grow for ever dark?
Fain would we ask, yet dread to know,
The mystery of the final doom,
That waits on all who pass below
The dreary threshold of the tomb !

Fain would we ask, why groan the lands
Beneath unutterable woe,
Scourged by oppression's crimson hands,
As ages come and ages go !
Why baffled justice idly pleads,
Foiled by the frauds of fools and knaves,
Why priestcraft weaves her specious creeds,
To fetter superstition's slaves!

Why Dives yet the purple wears,
While Lazarus freezes in the cold,
Why Mammon self-sufficient bears
The world's idolatry of gold !

Why folly, as in olden time,
Feasts at a board profusely spread,
While genius pens immortal rhyme,
Yet asks in vain his daily bread!

Why honour, prematurely grey,
Untitled to the grave descends,
Why love and friendship speed away,
When fortune's transient favour ends!
Why famine-struck, upon his bed
Of straw, neglected worth expires,
Why freedom droops her languid head,
As wane her half-extinguished fires!

And must we ever watch and weep,
And vainly wait the coming day,
When vengeance, waking from his sleep,
Shall smite to earth these gods of clay?
When truth, long promised, rends in twain
The veil that clouds our mortal sight,
While peals through heaven's expanse again,
The dread behest—Let there be light!

O Thou! who canst alone uphold
This wavering, weak, distrusting heart,
Arise! and by Thy might unfold,
That which we only see in part;
Bid, as Thine hour of wrath draws near,
The wail of tribulation cease,
Wipe from each eye the frequent tear,
And give Thy suffering people peace!

THE WIDOW OF NAIN.

" And when the Lord saw her, He had compassion on her, and
said unto her, Weep not."—Luke vii, 13.

FORTH from the city gate,
As evening shadows lengthen o'er the plain,
And the hushed crowd in reverent silence wait,
Passed out a funeral train.

Only one mourner there,
Slowly, with feeble steps, following the dead,
In the sad travail of the soul's despair
Bowed down her stricken head.

For him she wept forlorn,
Of care the solace, and of age the stay,
Whose silver chord was broken ere the morn
Had brightened into day.

Thus hath it ever been,
Time the destroyer sweeps relentless by,
When hopes are strong, and leaves of promise green,
And manhood's heart beats high.

Who comes, of stately mien,
As one with travel weary, seeking rest,
Whose aspect gentle and whose brow serene,
    Speak of a mission blest?

'Tis He, with power to save,
Who where desponding grief his vigil kept,
Knowing all human sufferings, at the grave
    Of Lazarus wept.

Thus spake He—" Weep no more !
Be still, sad heart !—be dry, ye moistened eyes !
Thus to the living I the dead restore;
    Sleeper, awake—arise ! "

Then at His bidding came
To those cold lips the warm returning breath ;
Then did He kindle life's extinguished flame,
    Victor o'er Sin and Death.

And thus He ever stands,
Friend of the fallen, wiping all tears away,
Wherever sorrow lifts her suppliant hands,
    And Faith remains to pray.

Where'er the wretched flee,
From the rude conflict of this world distrest,
Consoling words He whispers, "Come to me,
And I will give you rest."

Till at the second birth,
He bids the wrongs and woes of ages cease,
And brings to an emancipated earth,
Judgment and truth and peace.

And gathers all His own,
From the four winds to that eternal shore,
Where Mercy sits upon the great white throne,
And Death shall be no more.

LAYS OF THE SANCTUARY.

LAST THOUGHTS ON THE OLD YEAR.

HERE by my hearthstone lonely as I sit,
Watching the yule log glimmer through the gloom,
While ever and anon dark shadows flit,
Like youth's departing hopes across the room ;
In my deep reverie I essay to count,
The sum of all my years, and days, and hours,
And Time's unceasing river I remount,
To that pure fount where childhood gathered flowers ;
Thence tracing down through many weary ways,
The after current of life's ruffled stream,
Amidst the past regretful memory strays,
Till melts in air the unsubstantial dream ;
But as I number o'er the loved and lost,
The priceless moments fled, uncultured all,
And high resolves by sin and sorrow crost,
Which my repentant tears would fain recall ;
The chimes deep-toned tell to the drowsy night,
That we must wrap the old year in his shroud,
And welcome in the new ; thus in their flight
The wingèd moments speed, crying aloud,

" Awake vain dreamer, ere thy day be spent !
Thine is the common lot, gather thy strength,
And suffer and endure ; to thee is lent
This brief existence, that through grief at length,
Thy spirit purified from earthly care,
And having learnt with patient faith to bear
The Cross, shall wear at last the martyr's prize,
A starry crown and rest beyond the skies !"

LIST OF SUBSCRIBERS.

			No. of Copies.
Acland, Sir T. D., Bart.	...	Killerton	... 6
Acland, T. D., Esq. ...	...	Broadclist	... 2
Acland, W. H., Esq. ...	...	Bideford	... 1
Alldridge, Capt., R.N....	...	Pembroke	... 1
Baker, B., Esq. ...	...	London	... 1
Barber, W., Esq. ...	...	London	... 2
Barnard, I. F., Esq. ...	...	Barnstaple	... 1
Barry, Mr. J.	...	Barnstaple	.. 1
Bartlett, H., Esq. ...	...	Totness	.. 1
Barton, H. D., Esq. ...	...	Exeter	... 1
Bates, John, Esq. ...	...	Bristol	... 1
Bates, Spence, Esq. ...	...	Plymouth	... 1
Bawden, Rev. J. ...	...	Southmolton	... 1
Bazalgette, I. V. N., Esq.	...	London	... 1
Beadon, Mrs.	...	Highlands	... 1
Beadon, E., Esq. · ...	...	Highlands	... 1
Beadon, R., Esq. ...	...	Taunton	... 1
Beattie, I. H., Esq. ...	...	London	... 2
Bellerby, J., Esq. ...	...	Exeter	... 1
Bencraft, L., Esq. ...	...	Barnstaple	... 6
Bencraft, I., Esq. ...	...	Barnstaple	... 2
Bencraft, S., Esq. ...	...	Instow	... 1
Bencraft, H., Esq. ...	...	Southampton	... 1
Benham, Mr. G. C. ...	...	Barnstaple	... 1
Bere, Rev. C.	...	Uplowman	... 1
Bere, Montague, Esq. ...	...	London	... 6
Bidder, G. P., Esq., Pres. I.C.E.	London	... ...	... 6

K

Binford, Mrs.	Southmolton	...
Bird, W., Esq.	London	...
Bowdoin, J. Temple, Esq. ...	London	...
Bowring, Sir J., K.B.	Exeter ...	...
Brady, Mr. J.	Barnstaple	...
Braginton, G., Esq.	Torrington	...
Brailey, G., Esq.	Bideford	...
Brassey, T., Esq.	London	...
Bremridge, R., Esq.	Barnstaple	...
Bridges, H., Esq.	Bridgewater	...
Bridport, Lord...	Cricket...	...
Britton, Mr. W.	Barnstaple	...
Bromham, J. F., Esq.	Barnstaple	...
Brooman, R. A., Esq.	Twickenham	...
Brown, G., Esq.	Barnstaple	...
Brunel, Mrs.	London	...
Brunel, J., Esq.	London	...
Brutton, Mrs.	Northernhay	...
Brutton, Miss	Northernhay	...
Brutton, W. C., Esq.	London	...
Buckingham, W., Esq. ...	Exeter ...	...
Buller, J. W., Esq., M.P. ...	Downes	...
Burgess, M., Esq.	London	...
Burridge, W., Esq.	Wellington	...
Buse, R., Esq.	Bideford	...
Cammill, C., Esq.	London	...
Carew, John, Esq.	Exeter ...	...
Carwithen, Rev. J. C.	Challacombe	...
Chanter, J. R., Esq.	Barnstaple	...
Chanter, T. B., Esq.	Bideford	...
Chanter, T. S., Esq., R.N. ...	Plymouth	...
Chapman, Col. F., C.B., R.E...	Aldershott	...
Chapman, T., Esq., F.R.S. ...	London	...
Churston, Lord	Lupton...	...
Clarke, Capt. J. W.	London	...

				No. of Copies.
Clarke, E., Esq...	... ...	Chard ...	... ...	... 4
Clarke, W. W., Esq. ...	...	Cambridge	... ...	... 2
Clarke, H. W., Esq. ...	...	Exeter ...	... ...	... 6
Clarke, Mrs. ...	... ...	Exeter ...	... ...	... 1
Clarke, R. H., Esq. ...	...	Bridwell	... ...	... 1
Clarke, T. E., Esq. ...	...	Tremlett	... ...	... 1
Clarke, Master J. D. ...	...	Tremlett	.. ...	... 1
Clarke, S., Esq...	... ...	London	... ...	... 1
Clarke, R. I., Esq.	... ...	London	... ...	... 1
Clase, I., Esq. ...	... ...	Devonport	... ...	... 1
Clay, Sir W., Bart. ...	...	Fulwell Lodge	... ...	... 1
Clay, J. S., Esq...	... ...	Barnstaple	... ...	... 1
Cockshott, F., Esq. ...	...	Plymouth	... ...	... 1
Cohen, H. I., Esq	... ...	London	... ...	... 1
Collins. R. G., Esq. ...	...	Collumpton	... ...	... 1
Copeland, Mr. J.	... ...	Barnstaple	... ...	... 1
Cornish, Mr. T...	... ...	Barnstaple	... ...	... 1
Cornish, Mrs. ...	... ...	Barnstaple	... ...	... 1
Cornish, Mr. W.	... ...	Brighton	... ...	... 2
Cornish, Mr. J....	... ...	London	... ...	... 1
Cotton, E., Esq...	... ...	London	... ...	... 1
Crampton, T. R., Esq....	...	London	... ...	... 3
Cresswell, G. F., Esq. ...	...	Plymouth	... ...	... 1
Crombie, L., Esq. ...	...	London	... ...	... 1
Crosse, R. R., Esq. ...	...	Collumpton	... ...	... 1
Crosse, R. I., Esq. ...	...	Southmolton ...	... ...	... 1
Crosse, A. C., Esq. ...	...	Chapel-el-ne-frith	... ...	... 1
Cumming, G. W., Esq...	...	Exeter ...	... ...	... 1
Dakyn, Rev. W. Y. ...	...	Stoke Fleming	... ...	... 1
Dames, I. L., Esq. ...	...	Southmolton ...	... ...	... 1
Davy, Capt. I. T. ...	...	Roseash	... ...	... 1
Davie, Sir H. F., Bart., M.P...	Creedy ...	... ...	... 2
Davie, Col. I. D. F., M.P. ...	London	... ...	... 2
Daw, John, Esq. ...	...	Exeter ...	... ...	... 1
Deane, W., Esq. ...	...	Webbery	... ...	... 6

Dene, H., Esq.	Barnstaple	...
Dene, Rev. O......	Barnstaple	...
Denton, C., Esq.	London	...
Dewrance, J., Esq.	Peckham	...
Distin, A. S., Esq.	Totnes ...	...
Divett, E., Esq., M.P.... ...	Bystock	...
Drage, B. I., Esq.	London	...
Drake, C. C., Esq.	Barnstaple	...
Drew, J., Esq., Jun.	Powderham	...
Drew, H., Esq....	Peamore	...
Duins, T., Esq....	The Parks	..
Dunn, T., Esq.	Manchester	...
Edmonds, T. H., Esq.	Totnes ...	...
Edwards, H., Esq.	Bridgewater	...
Edwards, Rev. H.	Churchstanton	
Edwards, J. L., Esq... ...	Barnstaple	...
Edwards, G. H., Esq.	London	...
Elliott, Miss	Islington	...
Else, R. C., Esq.	Bridgewater	...
England, John, Esq.	London	...
Eveniss, G. A., Esq.	London	...
Everitt, G. A., Esq.	Birmingham	...
Errington, J. E., Esq.... ...	London	...
Fairlie, R. F., Esq.	London	...
Farnfield, W., Esq.	London	...
Fenning, G., Esq.	London	...
Fenwick, Capt.	High Bickington	
Flood, G. H., Esq.	London	...
Force, S. R., Esq......... ...	Exeter ..	...
Forrester, H., Esq., M.D. ...	Barnstaple	...
Fortescue, The Earl ...	Castle Hill	...
Foster, S. L., Esq.	Walsall	...
Fothergill, B. Esq.	Kennington	...
Freeman, R., Esq., M.D. ...	Plymouth	...

		No. of Copies.
Freeman, J., Esq.	London	... 1
Frend, E., Esq....	London	... 1
Froude, W., Esq.	Paignton	... 3
Fulford, R., Esq.	North Tawton ...	... 1
Furse, Rev. C. W.	Torrington	... 3
Galbraith, W. R., Esq. ...	Exeter	... 1
Gamble, C. H., Esq.	Barnstaple	... 1
Gilbert, P. I., Esq.	Bristol	... 1
Glyn, Major	Bideford	... 1
Gooch, D., Esq.	Reading	... 1
Gossett, Rev. I. H.	Northam	... 1
Gossett, A., Esq.	Northam	... 1
Gould, Mr. R. D.	Barnstaple	... 1
Graves, Lord	Plymouth	... 1
Gregory, Charles Hutton, Esq., Vice-Pres. Inst. C.E. ...	London	... 6
Gregory, Mr. T. D.	Barnstaple	... 1
Gribble, W., Esq.	London	... 1
Gribble, Miss	Barnstaple	... 1
Gribble. H. I., Esq.	Barnstaple	... 1
Guard, Rev. J.	Langtree	... 1
Guppy, T. W., Esq.	Barnstaple	... 1
Haviland, Hon. T. H.... ...	Prince Edward's Island	... 1
Hallinan, Mr. D.	Barnstaple	... 1
Hansard, O., Esq.	London	... 1
Hancock, Capt. W.	Wiveliscombe	... 4
Hanson, Alfred, Esq.	London	... 1
Harding, T. G., Esq.	Bideford	... 1
Hare, S. V., Esq.	Clifton	... 2
Hare, J., Esq.	Clifton	... 1
Harkness, J. M., Esq.... ...	London	... 1
Harris, G. H., Esq.	London	... 1
Harrison, G., Esq.	Birkenhead	... 1
Harwood, W., Esq.	Bristol	... 1

		No. of Copies.
Hartley, F., Esq.	Bideford	1
Haslin, T., Esq., M.A.	London	1
Hay, G., Esq.	London	1
Haydon, G. H., Esq.	London	1
Heath, Mr. John	Totnes	1
Helder, W., Esq.	London	1
Helps, Dr.	London	1
Hemans, G. W., Esq.	London	1
Hennett, F., Esq.	Bridgewater	1
Henry, D. H., Esq.	Camden Town	1
Hill, Mr. I.	Barnstaple	1
Hillier, G. A., Esq.	London	1
Hood, Dr.	London	1
Hood, G. H., Esq.	London	1
Hogg, Capt. T.	Newton Tracey	1
Hole, Capt.	Beam	1
Hole, Chas., Esq.	Ebberly	1
Hole, C., Esq., Jun.	Bideford	1
Hooper, H. W., Esq	Exeter	1
Hunt. W., Esq.	Stonehouse	1
Huyshe, Rev. J., M.A.	Clisthydon	1
Jeffery, Mr. J.	Barnstaple	1
Jeffery, Mrs.	Barnstaple	1
Jeyes, F. F., Esq.	London	1
Jones, Mrs.	Northernhay	1
Jones, Winslow, Esq.	Exeter	1
Jones, H., Esq.	Wear Gifford	2
Keats, Mrs.	Bideford	1
Keats, Colonel	Wiveliscombe	2
Keats, Admiral	Bideford	1
Keating, Rev. J., M.A.	Stonehouse	1
Kennaway, Mark, Esq.	Exeter	2
Kennaway, W., Esq.	Exeter	1
Kennaway, G., Esq.	Exeter	1

						No. of Copies.
Kennaway, Miss	..	...	Exeter ...	..	...	... 1
King, N., Esq. ...	...	...	Exeter ...	...	...	... 1
Laidman, C. J., Esq. ...	...	Exeter ...	...	...	... 1
Lambert, W., Esq.	...	...	Exeter ...	...	...	... 1
Lane, M., Esq. ...	...	...	Reading	...	...	... 2
Langdon, Mrs. ...	...	...	Chard ...	...	...	... 1
Langdon, J. C., Esq. ...	...	Parrocks	...	...	... 3
Langdon, G , Esq.	..	...	Braunton	...	...	... 1
Langdon, W., Esq.	...	...	Crediton	...	...	... 1
Langworthy, Miss	...	...	Crediton	...	...	... 3
Latimer, T., Esq.	...	...	Exeter ...	...	...	... 1
Ley, I. P. Esq....	...	...	Teignmouth	...	...	... 1
Lee, Mr. F.	...	...	.. Bideford	...	...	... 1
Leigh, A., Esq. ...	...	...	Collumpton	...	...	... 1
Lewis, C., Esq. ...	...	...	Exeter ...	...	...	... 1
List, Mr. J.	...	...	... Barnstaple	...	...	... 1
Lloyd, S., Esq. ...	...	...	Wednesbury	...	...	... 3
Lloyd, A., Esq. ..	...	...	Dartmouth	...	...	... 1
Lock, T., Esq. ...	...	...	Instow ...	...	...	... 1
Locke, A. T., Esq.	...	...	Dulverton	...	...	... 1
Locke, Joseph, Esq., M.P., F.R.S.	London	...	...	... 6
Long, W. H., Esq.	...	...	Exeter ...	...	...	... 6
Lopes, H. C., Esq.	...	...	London	...	...	... 1
Loveridge, Mrs.	...	...	Chard ...	...	...	... 1
Macartney, Major	...	...	Torrington	...	...	... 1
Mallett, J., Esq.	...	...	Instow ...	...	...	... 1
Manby, C , Esq., F.R.S.	...	London	...	...	... 2
Margary, P. L., Esq. ...	...	Dawlish	...	...	... 3
Marsh, James, Esq.	...	...	Exeter ...	...	...	... 1
Marsh, Mr. J. ...	...	...	Barnstaple	...	...	... 1
Marshall, B. M., Esq....	...	Mount Sandford	...	... 2
Marshall, Mrs....	...	...	Barnstaple	...	...	... 1
Marshall, Miss S.	...	...	Barnstaple	...	...	... 1
Marshall, Miss ...	...	...	Barnstaple	...	...	... 1

Marshall, E., Esq.   ...   ...   Birmingham ...
Martin, Mrs. ...   .   Barnstaple   ...
Maxwell, J., Esq.   ...   ...   Bydown   ...
McLean, J., Esq., Vice-Pres. I.C.E. London   ...
McVeagh, J., Esq.   ...   ...   London
Mears, W., Esq.   ...   ...   Exeter ...   ...
Melhuish, W., Esq.   ...   ...   Dawlish   ...

Northcote, H., Esq.   ...   ...   Okefield   ...

Ogilvie, A., Esq.   ...   ...   London   ...
Ogilvie, R., Esq.   ...   ...   Barnstaple   ...
Oliver, J., Esq. ...   .   London   ...
Osborne, Charles Stanley, Esq.   London   ...
Orton, S. A., Esq.   ..   ...   Barnstaple   ...

Page, T., Esq. ...   .   Tower Cressy ...
Palmer, W. G., Esq. ...   ...   Exeter ...   ...
Palmer, C. E., Esq. ...   ...   Barnstaple   ...
Parfitt, Dr.   ...   .   London   ...
Parsons, Mrs. ...   .   Ceylon ...   ...
Pascoe, J., Esq...   ...   ...   Barnstaple   ...
Patey, Mrs.   ...   .   Barnstaple   ...
Payne, E. W., Esq.   ...   ...   Salthill   ...
Pearse, J., Esq.   ...   ...   Southmolton ...
Pearse, J. G., Esq.   ...   ..   Southmolton ...
Poltimore, Lord, ...   Poltimore   ...
Portsmouth, The Earl of,   ...   Eggesford   ...
Postlethwaite, W., Esq.   ...   London   ...
Poulett, The Countess,   ...   Hinton St. George
Powning, Rev. J.   ...   ...   Totnes ...   ...
Price, W. G., Esq.   ...   ...   Torrington   ...
Pridham, Mr. W.   ...   ...   Barnstaple   ...
Pyke, B., Esq. ...   .   Bideford   ...

Redman, J. B., Esq. ...   ...   London   ...

		No. of Copies.
Reynolds, G., Esq.	South Yeo	1
Riccard, J. E., Esq.	Southmolton	2
Riccard, R., Esq.	Southmolton	1
Richards, W. J., Esq.	Exeter	1
Ridgway, Capt. A.	Shepleigh Blackawton	6
Ridgway, Mrs. A.	Shepleigh	2
Ridgway, A. F., Esq.	Shepleigh	1
Ridgway, T. G., Esq.	Shepleigh	1
Ridgway, Miss Alice	Shepleigh	1
Ridgway, P., Esq., 98th Regt.	Kurracheo	1
Ridgway, Miss G.	Barnstaple	1
Rigby, E., Esq.	London	1
Risk, Rev. J. Erskine	Plymouth	1
Roberts, Mrs.	Westleigh	1
Rock, W. F., Esq.	London	4
Rodd, R. R., Esq.	Stonehouse	1
Rooker, J., Esq.	Bideford	1
Rowe, Mr. A.	Barnstaple	1
Russell, J. Scott, Esq., F.R.S.	London	2
Russell, Rev. J.	Swimbridge	1
Salter, W., Esq.	Chard	1
Saunders, W. W., Esq.	London	1
Saunders, W., Esq.	London	1
Savile, E. B., Esq.	Barnstaple	1
Sellwood, B., Esq.	Cullompton	1
Seth, Mrs.	B. Salterton	1
Sillifant, J., Esq.	Coombe	1
Sillifant, Rev. C. W.	Wear Gifford	1
Simpson, W., Esq.	London	6
Sharland, W., Esq.	Exmouth	1
Sharpe, M., Esq.	London	1
Slight, F., Esq.	London	1
Stoley, J., Esq.	Torrington	1
Smith, Montague, Esq., M.P.	London	1
Smith, T. M., Esq.	Bideford	1

Smith, F., Esq....	Crediton	...
Smith, P., Esq., M.D. ...	London	...
Smith, W. Castle, Esq.	London	...
Smith, W., Esq.	London	...
Smyth, W. G., Esq. ...	Southmolton	...
Snow, B., Esq.	Glastonbury	...
Soltau, G. W., Esq. ...	Efford	...
Sparkes, P., Esq. ...	Exeter	...
Spicer, Miss F.... ...	Chard ...	...
Spinkes, D., Esq. ...	Bridgewater	...
Stancombe, Mrs. ...	Clifton	...
Stevens, J. M., Esq. ...	Winscott	...
Strapp, J., Esq. ...	Surbiton	...
Surgey, J. B., Esq. ...	London	...
Sydenham, Rev. J. B ...	Cullompton	...
Tabb, Mr. W. S. ...	Barnstaple	...
Tamlyn, J., Esq. ...	Barnstaple	...
Tanner, W., Esq. ...	Exeter ...	...
Tarr, R., Esq.	Trowbridge	...
Tatham, Mr. J. W. ...	Barnstaple	...
Tayler, S., Esq. ...	London	...
Thomas, Capt.	Instow	...
Thompson, Rev. A. K , D.D...	Bideford	...
Thompson, J., Esq. ...	Bideford	...
Thompson, W. H., Esq. ...	London	...
Thorne, Mr. H. K. ...	Barnstaple	...
Thorne, W., Esq. ...	Barnstaple	...
Tite, W., Esq. M.P., F.R S. ...	London	...
Tolmè, J. H., Esq. ...	London	...
Tombs, W., Esq ...	Exeter ...	...
Torr, Mrs. J.	Westleigh	...
Torr, Mrs. G.	Torville	...
Tripe, L. P., Esq. ...	Devonport	...
Trobridge, Miss ...	Islington	...
Truscott, G., Esq. ...	Exeter ...	...

			No. of Copies.
Tucker, T. P., Esq.	Barnstaple		1
Turner, Charles, Esq.	Exeter		1
Tyrrell, J., Esq.	Newcourt		6
Tyrrell, G. N., Esq.	London		1
Tyrrell, J., Esq., Jun.	Ide		1
Tudbail, Rev. T.	Teignmouth		1
Valletort, Lord, M.P.	Plymouth		2
Vaughan, Hugh, Esq.	Barnstaple		1
Vellacott, Mr. J.	Bideford		1
Vellacott, Mr. W.	Bideford		1
Vidal, E. U., Esq.	Bideford		1
Waghorn, Mr.	Taunton		1
Walrond, J. W., Esq.	Bradfield		3
Ward, Elias T, Esq.	Langridge		2
Warren, H. G., Esq.	London		1
Webb, C. L., Esq.	London		3
Webster, Miss	Southernhay		1
Wellington, Rev. W.	Upton Helyons		3
Wescomb, Chas., Esq.	Exeter		1
Wesseles, H. W., Esq.	London		1
Wheeler, J. F., Esq.	Cardiff		1
Whichcord, J., Esq.	London		1
Whidborne, J., Esq.	Teignmouth		6
White, E., Esq.	London		1
White, R., Esq.	Instow		2
White, E. M., Esq.	Bideford		1
Whitmarsh, Rev. W.	H.M.S. Implacable		1
Whitter, T W., Esq.	Cullompton		1
Whitter, Miss Ada	Cullompton		1
Whitter, W, Esq.	Bridford		1
Wickham, W., Esq.	Bideford		1
Willcock, S., Esq.	Bideford		1
Willcocks, W., Esq.	Alphington		1
Williams, Mr. J.	Appledore		1

			No. of Copies.
Williams, Mr. W. H. ...	...	Bideford	... 1
Wills, M., Esq....	...	... London	... 1
Woods, Captain	...	... Exeter	... 1
Wollacott, Mr. J.	...	... Barnstaple	... 1
Woolmer, Mrs. J.	...	... Barnstaple	... 1
Wren, Major ...	...	... Linwood	... 1
Wren, A., Esq....	....	... Bradworthy	... 1
Wright, J., Esq.	...	... Birmingham	... 1
Yarde, Mrs. ...	...	... Trowbridge House ...	... 2
Yeatman Rev. H. F., B.C.L. ...		·Sherborne	... 1
Yelland, R. E., Esq. ...		... Bideford	... 1
Young, W., Esq.	...	... Instow	... 1
Zetland, Earl of	...	... London	... 1

J. B. BATEMAN, PRINTER, 1, IVY LANE, PATERNOSTER ROW, LONDON.

ADDENDA.